Greetings from the s

I hope you enjoy rea..ectra
Brown, *Taking the Plu*

Electra takes the plunge and accepts Claudia Barnes' bet that she won't go out with the first boy who asks her, but her date isn't exactly the stuff of her dreams. Her friends have their own problems, too – Lucy's past comes back to haunt her and Sorrel's world becomes a nightmare. As Electra faces up to the grim consequences of her actions, she still can't stop those shallow thoughts surfacing. Does she really fancy a four-cheese pizza more than a Spanish Lurve God?

I'm often asked whether these books are based on real people and real life. Although the characters are fictitious, they *are* based on people I've met, and all the mad, bad and sad happenings are taken from real-life situations. Whilst at school I used to sit and stare out of the window at school dreaming of *anything* but lessons, then go home and write pages and pages in my diary of who did what to whom, and (usually) why wasn't I part of it? Years later, that dreaming and those diaries are brought to life through Electra and her friends.

With love,

Helen

X

About the Author

Helen Bailey was born and brought up in Ponteland, Newcastle-upon-Tyne. Barely into her teens, Helen invested her pocket money in a copy of *The Writers' and Artists' Yearbook* and spent the next few years sending short stories and poems to anyone she could think of. Much to her surprise, she sometimes found herself in print. After a degree in science, Helen worked in the media and now runs a successful London-based character licensing agency handling internationally renowned properties such as Dirty Dancing, Dilbert and Felicity Wishes. With her husband, John, she divides her time between Highgate, north London and the north-east. She is the author of a number of short stories, young novels and picture books.

www.helenbaileybooks.com

TAKING THE PLUNGE

Helen Bailey

Hodder
Children's
Books

A division of Hachette Children's Books

For Christie Rochester, with love

The shallows of Electra Brown's life:

www.helenbaileybooks.com

Chapter One

'It's a bomb, not a bra,' I announce as I carefully place a large parcel wrapped in brown paper on the table, and plonk my butt on a chair opposite Lucy.

'No!' Luce gasps, backing away from the possible parcel bomb towards the wall and wrapping her hair around her face, as if a sheet of dead blonde protein is really going to protect her from flying shrapnel.

'Luce, she's joking,' Sorrel says coolly. 'If Electra *really* thought that was a bomb, do you honestly think she'd have brought it here and risked turning us into uncooked mince?'

I'd like to point out that firstly, we do everything together, and secondly, sitting opposite me, Sorrel doesn't look quite as cool as she thinks she does, sipping her cappuccino. She's got a quivering milk mouche covering her upper lip and a huge blob of chocolate powder on the end of her nose.

We've given up meeting in Burger King or Macky D's on Saturday mornings for three reasons:

One, both places have been invaded by shrieking junior runts from our school.

Two, now we're older, we've decided it's about time we became more sophisticated and sipped designer coffees in Starbucks, rather than make farting noises by bubbling air through the straw in our milkshakes.

And three, and the main reason for our change of weekend hangout, Sorrel says even the smell of cremated flesh reminds her of ex-burger flipper, ex-Maccy D's employee and *very* ex-Lurve God, Warren Cumberbatch.

According to Sorrel, just the thought of him makes her want to instantly vom, and as no one wants a display of spontaneous public chundering (*so* off-putting when you're cramming your face with food), and Starbucks sells sarnies rather than steaks, here seems the safest choice.

The whole Warren–Sorrel thing was always going to end in tears, though we never thought it would end up with him lusting after Sorrel's sexy older sister, Jasmine, and using Sorrel as a way to get to her. But Sorrel wouldn't listen when we told her that a free burger by the rat-infested bins didn't count as a hot date. Now she veers between feeling heartbroken and off her food, to fantasizing about sticking a skewer into the louse, putting him in front of a hot flame and turning him into a giant doner kebab.

Still, the anti-meat phase is pleasing Yolanda Callender, Sorrel's rampantly vegan mother, though I don't think Sorrel has made it clear that her current meat-free status is because she wants to flame-grill a teenage boy, rather than because she's concerned about animal welfare.

Lucy's still looking a bit freaked by the sight of the potentially explosive parcel, but has unwrapped her face and is now leaning over the table, staring at the package.

'Who hates you enough to blow you up?' she asks. 'Who've you upset recently?'

There could be so many people, but the evidence points to only one woman.

'The Kipper!' I hiss, pointing at the white address label on which *Electra Brown, 14 Mortimer Road* is scrawled in spidery blue ink. 'Caroline Cole! It's the handwriting of the devil and she wants revenge!'

I'd been mega-excited after school on Friday, when Mum handed me a red-and-white card saying the postman had tried to deliver a parcel whilst we were out. I was certain it was a Make The Most Of Your Minuscule Mammaries Miracle Air Bra that Maddy, my glam American Wundacousin, had promised to send me, a bra I so desperately need if I'm not to appear lopsided in the bap department for ever.

So, after a nice long Saturday morning lie-in, I'd got to the post office just before it shut at midday. But when the dry old stick with the thick tortoiseshell specs opened the glass window and handed me the parcel and I saw The Kipper's handwriting, not Maddy's, I realized it wasn't a miracle-performing bap-pack from New York after all, but something nasty from my father's evil girlfriend – if not a bomb, perhaps a box of beetle dung, itching powder or decaying rats.

Caroline Cole might look like a dead smoked fish (bony, fake-tan orange skin, dead glassy eyes, reeks of stale fags), but Dad's current girlfriend is really a very much alive and dangerous piranha, a man-eating gold-digger only after Dad's money, out to trap him into marrying her and getting her name double-barrelled on the platinum credit card.

When Mads was staying at half-term we even got video evidence of her evil plan, *and* proof that she loathes me. But as I couldn't bear to upset Dad by confronting him with the facts, and The Kipper wanted more time to flash his cash, I made a pact with her. I won't tell Dad she's a gold-digging bully if eventually she admits to him she hates his kids and wishes me and my little bro Jack, aka The Little Runt, had never been born, at which point I'm pretty sure Dad will bin her. It's much better to be the dumper than the dumpee, and this way I reckon Dad's heart won't be quite so broken.

I knew I'd made a pact with the she-Devil, but I hadn't counted on her wanting revenge so soon.

My moby rings and I look down to see Claudia Barnes's boobs flashing on its screen, still cracked from when I hurled it into a rack of T-shirts in a fit of parental-induced temper. Because of the whole shoulders-back, boobs-out look she always has, the girls and me secretly call Claudia Tits Out, so it seemed entirely normal to have furtively snapped her at the bus stop one morning and added the pic to my phone. Now I'm thinking of deleting it in case anyone sees a girl's chest on my moby – even one covered by a white shirt and green blazer – and thinks I have a touch of the lesbionics.

'Electra?'

'Yeah.'

'It's Claudia.'

'Yeah.'

'Is Lucy with you? She's not answering her phone.'

'She's here.'

'Where's here?'

'Starbucks at Eastwood.'

'Give me two mins.'

And then she rings off.

'What was all that about?' Luce asks as one of the Starbuckies eyes up our table.

One of the downsides of being here compared to BK or Macky D's is that they notice if you haven't ordered anything for hours, or get three straws with one drink and keep topping up your cup with free milk. No one has actually said anything yet, but that whole hovering-with-a-spray-bottle-and-cloth routine can be *very* intimidating.

'Tits Out is after you,' I say, taking a slurp of Lucy's coffee, a bitter espresso, which I feel takes the whole grown-up-beverage thing too far. 'She's on her way here. You weren't answering your moby.'

'I felt it vibrate but thought it was Mum,' Luce groans. 'She's been stressing me out over my birthday. Anyone would think it was her day, not mine.'

'I thought we were all going to that beauty place,' I say. 'Isn't it all arranged?'

Bella Malone had promised to treat Luce, me and Sorrel to an afternoon at Cloudz beauty salon for Lucy's fifteenth birthday next Saturday. It's going to cost a bomb, but probably not as much as it cost to put our house back together after my disastrous fourteenth birthday party, where the house *looked* as if it had been bombed, I got wrecked, and our guinea pig, Google, ran away and ended up half eaten and buried in a pale-blue Tiffany box, which is probably why Bella wants us away from their house. Given that she stresses out over stray pubes on the bathroom floor, even a tiny scratch on their polished wood table could tip the Neat Freak into a mental meltdown.

'Oh, don't say your mum's changed her mind?' I moan, gutted that I won't be pampered at Bella's expense. 'I was planning on being fake-tanned all over.'

'She's now talking about taking me for a posh meal at Giovanni's,' Luce says, rolling her eyes. '*Without* you two.'

Bella has made it quite clear she thinks I'm a bad influence on her daughter, but surely even she knows I'm not going to run riot in a beauty salon. What does she think I'm going to do? Start rampaging with wax strips? Throw mudpacks around? Turn up the voltage on the electrolysis machine and electrocute people?

'So, is Saturday on or off?' Sorrel asks. 'Please say on or I'll be lumbered with babysitting the kids *again*.'

'I've said I'm not putting a foot inside Giovanni's unless you come too,' Luce says. '*And* I want a pamper party.'

Since Luce got help for her self-harm issues earlier this year she's started to stand up to her mum a bit more, though I'm not sure that stamping your feet and demanding two parties counts as progress, just stroppiness.

'Hiya!'

Claudia Barnes comes trotting through the door. She sits next to Lucy and unzips her puffy silver coat to reveal a tiny pink spaghetti-strapped top, from under which pokes a lacy red satin bra. As she tries to release her arms from the silver tubes her boobs jiggle alarmingly, and I wonder which will pop out of her top first, a natural boob or a chicken fillet, and, not for the first time, feel totally freaked that I find Tits Out's boobs so fascinating.

Claudia elbows Lucy in the ribs.

'Luce, guess what? I've just seen Naz Ashri, you know, lower sixth, would be lush if he didn't have a wonky eye? Anyway Naz let slip that Josh Caldwell fancies you, but when I snogged Josh last summer at the Year 11 leavers' do he was a crap kisser, such stiff lips he was practically dead, which is tragic as he's total eye candy. Anyway, I thought I'd better warn you first.'

I didn't know Claudia had snogged Josh Caldwell, though I'm not surprised. She seems to have snogged *everyone* with a Y chromosome. I'm gutted to find out that what I thought was one of the sixth formers winking at me is really down to a dodgy eye.

Lucy doesn't seem impressed that a sixth former who kisses like a corpse and has snogged Tits Out fancies her.

I'd be impressed that *anyone* fancies me, even one with paralysed lips gasping his last breath.

'What's that?' Tits Out asks, pointing at the package on the table.

'It's a bomb,' Sorrel says sarkily, probably hoping that the threat of an explosive device in Starbucks will have Tits Out clambering for the door and leave us in peace.

'You've got a chocolate beak,' Claudia tells Sorrel, who glares at Tits Out and furiously rubs her nose clean of brown powder. 'No, really. What is it?'

'It's something my dad's girlfriend sent me,' I explain before the hovering Starbucky with the sprayer overhears us and, fearing that we're a group of teenage fundamentalists, calls the bomb squad. 'She hates me so I was sort of half joking she'd mailed a bomb.'

'Well, go on, open it,' Tits Out says. 'See what it is.'

I know it's not a bomb, but even so, as I'm tearing off the brown paper, my heart starts hammering and my hands shake a little, though that could be due to the caffeine shot from Lucy's espresso.

Under the brown paper is a cardboard box with *Baby Wipes* printed along the side in blue ink.

'I knew it!' I shriek, pushing the package away. 'That is *so* typical of that evil witch. What sort of a woman sends a teenager a box of baby bum wipes through the post?

What's she implying? That I'm still a sprog? That I have a dirty backside? What?'

I'm so busy ranting about The Kipper and her totally inappropriate and disappointing choice of present, I don't notice anything going on around me until I hear all three girls gasp.

'It's not a bomb!' Luce squeals excitedly.

'Wicked,' Sorrel says.

'Blimey!' Tits Out squeals.

The Kipper hasn't sent me a box of baby botty cloths.

Buried amongst scrunched up pages from *heat* magazine is a cream cotton bag, and peeping out of the top like a newly laid egg is The Kipper's pale-cream Chloé bling bag I'd lusted after. The evil witch had taunted me with it, pretending I could borrow it but then denying she'd ever mentioned it. And now, here it is, in front of me, on a table in Starbucks.

'You lucky cow,' Tits Out says, reaching over to stroke the soft leather, which makes me wince, as I'm terrified one of her French-manicured talons will scratch it. 'It's much too lush to be fake.'

'There has to be a catch,' I say as I put all our cups on the next table, wipe the surface with my jacket sleeve and carefully lift The Bag of Beauty from its paper nest and soft cotton casing. 'I can't believe she'd do this otherwise.'

I open up the bag and, to be honest, instead of the smell of expensive leather it reeks of perfume and stale cigarette smoke. Still, it's nothing a bottle of Febreze and an airing in the garden won't solve.

'Keep well away,' Sorrel growls at a Starbucky who has come dangerously close to The Bag of Beauty with a cloth and a bottle of purple liquid. 'Damage that bag and we'll sue you!'

The Starbucky scuttles off, leaving us to coo and stroke the newborn bag, playing with the gold padlock and fingering its dangly bits.

'I'd do anything for a bag like that,' Tits Out says, practically drooling at the sight of The Bag of Beauty. 'How much do you want for it?'

'As if, Claudia!' I snort. I can't believe The Kipper's given me a bling bag costing *hundreds* of pounds. 'Nothing would make me give up this bag. *Nothing.*'

'Everything has a price,' Sorrel says, examining a red glass bead on the end of one of her braids. 'Depends on whether what you're being offered is more valuable than what you have already.'

'If Claudia offered you five thousand pounds you'd take it,' Lucy says, showing surprising insight. 'Then you could buy loads of bling bags.'

'If I could afford five grand I'd buy my own bling bag,'

Claudia retorts. 'Go on, what do I have that you want more than that bag?'

I look at The Queen of Sleaze with her ironed-straight bleached hair, dodgy boobs and purple badges of slaggery circling her neck. I'd like to be as popular with the boys as Claudia, but not if it meant I had a reputation as a bit of a tart, even one with a good heart.

I'm still thinking when Claudia says, 'Name one thing you really really lust after.'

'Jags?'

I love Luce to bits. We've known each other since first year of infants. Along with Sorrel, she's my best friend. But right now I could cheerfully reach across the table and slap her with one of the dangly bits on The Bag of Beauty, not because she's let slip a secret, but because Jags is *so* last term.

Yes, despite spending thousands of hours dreaming about splashing in foaming white surf, or running through golden cornfields hand in hand with the Spain-via-Slough Lurve God, I'm wondering if he really is a squat, over-gelled, greasy little munchkin, which was Maddy's opinion when she met him.

'*You* fancy *Jags*?' Claudia sounds gobsmacked. 'Javier Antonio Garcia Jags?' She blows air out of her mouth and her fringe flies up to reveal a fine collection of glowing forehead zits. 'I never guessed. I know Jags *really* well.'

I bet you do, I think.

I still can't forget that after my disaster party I could smell Claudia's chavvy perfume on my duvet, and that at some point during it, Jags was outside my bedroom door. I know he was outside my bedroom door because that's where I collapsed at his feet, having pulled his jeans down as I sank on to the green carpet, totally wasted on coloured buzz juice.

'I used to think he was OK,' I shrug, trying to look casual. 'Just 'cause he was a bit foreign and better than the berks at Burke's.'

'Even Frazer Burns?' Claudia says suggestively, raising an overplucked eyebrow.

I can feel my face burn and contemplate putting the Chloé dust bag over my head as an embarrassed-face disguise.

'Pinhead said he saw you and FB holding hands on Talbot Road last week.' Claudia obviously isn't going to let this one drop. 'I thought you two might be secret snoggers.'

'As if!' I gasp, hoping that the Starbucky with the sprayer will throw us out to cut the conversation. 'Me and Razor Burns? Get real, Claudia!'

'So Pinhead was lying?' She leans across the table

towards me. I expect she's trying to eyeball me, but I'm ignoring her over-made-up eyes and looking down, fiddling with The Bag of Beauty's bits and pieces. 'And Gibbo? And Spud? They all said they'd seen you and him with meshed mitts. Are they *all* lying?'

I give a deep *Do I really have to explain?* type sigh.

'FB was giving his dog, Archie, a bath and Archie got out so we ran after him. FB just grabbed my hand to make sure I kept up.'

This sounds convincing because it's the truth, though it doesn't explain what I was doing at FB's house in the first place. I also don't add that we held hands for slightly longer than was necessary and that the only reason we let go was because FB had rushed out without the dog's lead or collar, and to avoid the mutt playing Dodge That Car in the traffic and causing a pile-up, FB had to carry him home. Then the moment was lost; he took the wet dog inside, and I scurried back and wrote *EB 4 FB* in a heart on my maths book, something which turned out to be a mega mistake, as even after nuking it with half a bottle of Tippex you can still see the design if you hold it up to the light.

Since then, neither of us has said anything to each other.

'Hmm . . .' Claudia is clearly unconvinced that I'm not having a passionate affair behind her back.

14

'Would you go out with FB if he asked you?' Lucy pipes up.

This is a difficult question.

On the one hand, FB isn't known as Freak Boy for nothing. On the other, not many people have seen what I've seen, which is that FB can look *totally* hot, but only if he's drenched in water, just as he was the day I saw him with Archie. The problem with dating a Just Add Water boy is that I'd have to carry a bucket around with me and keep dousing him every time he was in danger of drying out. This would be embarrassing, restrict our choice of dating venues and might be awkward to explain, not just to people around, but to him.

'I don't think you'd go out with anybody,' Claudia says, sounding very sure of herself. 'Even if someone totally lush like Buff Butler asked you.'

'I would so!' I'm mad that Claudia is making wild assumptions about my non-existent love life, though slightly concerned that I seem to have agreed that I would go out with our gorge geography teacher, something that would get us both expelled from Flora Burke's Community School.

'Well, have you ever been out with anybody?' she asks. 'Even on a double-date?'

I throw Claudia what I hope is the sort of sarky look

that could mean anything from *Get lost* to *As if I'm going to tell you!*

It clearly doesn't work as she says, 'So you haven't then, even though everyone else has.' She elbows Lucy. 'You went out with that French lad, Pascal, didn't you?'

Luce wrinkles her nose at the thought of her summer-holiday fling with the blond bogbrush-headed Frog called Pascal Fournier who lives in Provence. When she first came back from France she was all *Ooh là là!* about him but, along with her tan, the romance faded and she no longer sighs and snogs the pictures of him on her phone.

'And you had a sort of thing with that lad who worked at Burger King.' Claudia nods towards Sorrel and I snatch the bag protectively towards me in case of sudden projectile vomiting in its direction.

'So it's just you, Electra. A dating virgin.'

'I'm choosy,' I say, wanting to point out that I'm not the only non-dater as Sorrel didn't actually go out with Warren, but I'm too scared to bring the subject up in case Sorrel brings up her cappuccino.

'You're not choosy!' Claudia trills, looking down and tucking something (a boob? a chicken fillet? her moby?) deeper into her cleavage. 'You're just too scared to take the plunge!'

'Crappola, Claudia.' I toss my hair in what I hope is a

suitably offhand manner rather than looking as if I'm about to have a fit. 'You're talking rubbish.'

It's true.

She is.

The reason I haven't been out with anybody isn't that I'm too scared to stick my lips into the dating pond, but that nobody has asked me.

Ever.

Claudia reaches across and pats The Bag of Beauty. 'I bet you this bag that you won't agree to go out with the first lad that asks you in the next two weeks. If you do, I'll get you a date with Jags. If you chicken out, I get the bag. Agreed?'

Ooh, my butterfly brain is flapping and my head is stressing!

I was *sure* I'd gone right off Jags, but if I did go out with him then I'd finally know whether I really *have* gone off him, or am merely off him because he's never been on me. And a date with The Spanish Lurve God would look fab on my dating CV. He might be a greasy little munchkin but he's a bit older, at another school, a *posh* school, and he's sort-of foreign, which gives him an exotic touch.

It's sooo tempting.

'And if no one asks me out?' I say. 'What then? Do I still keep the bag?'

'Yep,' Tits Out says, putting her coat back on and tucking her boobs in. 'But there's no Jags date. So, do we have a deal?'

As Claudia struggles to force the zip over her chest, I think for a moment. My brain is doing lots of calculations along the lines of past experience of being asked out (zero), versus future likelihood (unknown but probably zero) and so on. Maths isn't my strong point as Mrs Chopley, my Year 10 maths teacher, would tell you, but it doesn't take me long to come up with an answer.

'Agreed,' I say. Claudia sticks out her hand and we shake on it. 'You've got a deal.'

Chapter Two

The girls are *totally* shocked at the bet I've just made.

As we leave Starbucks and Claudia heads off to rendezvous with Natalie 'Butterface' Price by the Maybelline display in Superdrug, presumably so Nat can buy more greasy yellow slap, Lucy pipes up first.

'What have you done?' she gasps. 'You could lose that gorgeous bag!'

'Never going to happen, Luce,' I say confidently, ramming the Baby Bum Wipe box and packaging into a nearby bin and wondering if it will look odd if I have The Bag of Beauty slung over one arm and my usual Top Shop cheapie on the other.

'You hope,' mutters Sorrel as we head out into the freezing November air.

'Trust me, it won't,' I say, admiring my new bag as we pass shop windows. 'I've got Plan A and Plan B, and both of them mean I get to keep the bag and maybe get a bonus date with Jags.'

Both girls groan at the mere mention of the word *plan*.

'Oh, Electra, remember more of your plans go wrong than go right,' Lucy points out. 'You're still gambling with the Chloé.'

'Operation Catch A Kipper went well,' I say. 'Maddy and I found out Caroline Cole wasn't in fact a kipper, but a piranha.'

'And what about Operation Bald Eagle, The Party Plan, The Glam Plan, The Beat The Impostor Plan—'

'OK, OK,' I say, cutting Sorrel off before she can reel off any more of my famously disastrous plans. 'But there's no *way* this one can fail. Firstly, no one is going to ask me out because in fourteen years they haven't done, so it's hardly likely they're going to in the next two weeks, is it? And if by some miracle they do, then I'll say *Yes*, keep the bag, go out with Jags and win the bet. I tell you, girls, it's a win—win situation.'

'So if that's Plan A, what's Plan B?' Lucy asks.

'I'm still working on Plan B,' I say, not actually having a Plan B yet.

'So you haven't considered Plan C?' Sorrel asks.

'How can there be a Plan C when Plan B's not in place yet?' I reply, already stressing over what look I should adopt for my possible Jags date. I'm thinking slightly tarty, but with an intelligent classy edge.

Sorrel shakes her head. 'Plan C is Plan Claudia. Tits Out will get some plug-ugly lad with rank breath, sticky-out ears and grubby fingers to ask you out, knowing that you'll say no, just so she can get the bag.'

My stomach hits the floor, which, if I carry on eating so many Pop-Tarts and Snickers bars, may actually happen next time I get undressed.

'She wouldn't!' I shriek, knowing full well she would.

Claudia Barnes can charm any boy with her come-shag-me eyes and boobs on a plate, and if she's confident enough to get a boy like Jags to go out with a girl like me for a bet, she could easily get a Mega Minger with about-to-burst zits, braces and thick glasses to ask me out, in which case I'd be *totally* humiliated and my first date, the most important date in my life *so far*, would be spent freaking over whether one of the Mega Minger's zits was about explode and cover me in cheesy pus.

The humiliation wouldn't stop there.

Oh no.

It would get around that I'm a Mega Minger Dater so that all the other totally gross lads would think they have a chance with me and pester me for dates, whilst any reasonable lad would avoid me as I'd be contaminated by minger exposure, not to mention spot pus.

'I need a Plan B!' I'm practically hysterical. 'I've got to have a Plan B to stop Plan C. Help me with Plan B!'

By now we're standing under the hot-air vents just inside the entrance to Marks & Spencer. It's not the most glamorous of places, and it's really annoying when people with shopping trolleys piled with food make us move so they can get past, but it's dry and warm and will do as a hang-out until we get moved on by the security guards.

'You need to stay one step ahead of Tits Out and control the bet,' Sorrel says. 'Once you lose control, you're sunk. If you don't, you might as well give her the bag straightaway, unless of course you're prepared to go out with a Shrek Head.'

'As if, but how?' I say, trying to move away from the hot air as I'm quite hot enough at the thought of the mess I've got myself into, and completely freaked that Plan A has failed *instantly* and I'm now facing a lose–lose bet situation.

Sorrel leans against a row of trolleys, checking there are no coins stuck in the locks. 'You need to go out with someone *you* choose and *fast*. Beat Claudia to it. Oh, and steer clear of Shrek Heads and Mega Mingers until you do.'

'In case you've forgotten, I'm not Claudia Barnes!' I

squeak, pointing at my chest, which is buried somewhere deep beneath my black jacket. 'I can't just get a half-decent lad to ask me out at the drop of a hat!'

'This isn't a ruddy social club,' growls a voice I recognize. 'You're blocking the exit.'

'Dad!'

I'm amazed to see Dad coming out of M&S, wearing a woolly hat over his coot-head and clutching a carrier bag. He hates shopping as much as I hate aubergines and my wide face.

'Oh. Hello.' He looks surprised to see me. He nods at the girls who nod back. 'What are you lot doing here?'

If Dad paid any attention to my life he'd know that we're pretty much *always* at Eastwood on a Saturday afternoon, and often under the M&S air vents when it's cold.

'More like, what are *you* doing here?' I say. 'You hate shopping.'

'Needs must and all that,' he says, jiggling the carrier bag. 'I needed new supplies.'

'What's in there?' I ask, grabbing the bag off him and peering in. It seems to be a couple of microwaveable meals for one and some huge grey pants.

'Dad, is everything all right?' I ask, handing him back the bag.

The big pants, the saddo-meals, him being in M&S on a Saturday afternoon. Something feels wrong, but he just smiles and says, 'Fine. You?'

I swing my right shoulder round to show him The Bag of Beauty, swiping a wrinkly with the left-shoulder Top Shop cheapie.

'The Kip— Caroline sent me this, but I've no idea why, unless she can't bear to be seen with last year's model!'

'What am I looking at?' Dad says, and the girls giggle.

'The bag, Dad! The bag! Caroline's sent me a serious piece of designer leather! Will you thank her for me?'

I don't really want to thank her but I've been brought up to be polite, and anyway, it saves Mum bullying me into writing her a thank-you note, which might kill me.

'If you want to thank her, you'll have to thank her yourself,' Dad says rather sharply. 'Caroline and I are no longer an item.'

'Since when?' I gasp, thinking, *Since when did my dad start to use phrases like 'an item'?*

'Since about a week or so,' Dad says.

'What happened?' I ask.

'Fancy a coffee?' he replies.

We're sitting in the café in M&S, Dad with a strong black coffee, me with a milky hot chocolate and a packet of tiny triangular sandwiches with different fillings, The Bag of Beauty safely wrapped in my jacket in case of accidental chocolate-milk spillage.

The girls took the hint that Dad wanted to talk, so, after I whispered I'd text them with any Kipper-related info and made them promise to keep thinking about Plan B and outwitting Claudia's Plan C, they wandered off towards the cinema to see what was on.

'So, what happened?' I ask, struggling to undo the plastic case and release the sarnies.

'I'm still not really sure,' Dad says as a salmon and cucumber triangle falls out of the packet and drops on the floor.

So that some old relic doesn't slip on it and break their hip, I pick it up. Even blowing on it isn't going to get rid of the muck stuck to the brown bread, so I carefully put it to one side of my plate, and start on the others.

'One minute it was all fantastic, and then I just casually mentioned it might be nice if her and me and you and Jack went away together at Christmas and she went mental. Never seen a woman instantly change moods like that. Your mother never did. Completely flipped and started ranting.'

I nibble an egg and cress, which tastes nice but smells of toxic farts and dodgy loos.

'What did she say?'

Dad looks uncomfortable.

'Quite a lot actually, some of it really nasty, but the upshot was that she didn't want to spend her precious Christmas break stuck with a couple of children who weren't hers and that she didn't like.'

The Kipper did *keep to her side of the bargain*, I think to myself.

I have to say I'm surprised. I really thought she'd string the piranha act out a bit longer so she could carry on giving the credit cards a bashing, or even go back on our deal and start bullying me again. Walking to M&S, it had occurred to me that The Bag of Beauty might be part of some sort of blackmail plan she'd hatched. She'd let me fall in love with it, use it for weeks, and then say she'd tell Dad I'd stolen it if I told him about her money-making scheme and showed him the video evidence I've got copied on a CD and stashed in my underwear drawer.

Perhaps I misjudged her.

'So you split up?'

Dad nods. 'Of course we did. I'm not going to stand for that!'

I reach across the table and squeeze Dad's arm; a mistake, as I've smeared some eggy mayo on his jacket sleeve.

What with lying about his affair with Candy Baxter,

leaving Mum and then not believing me about The Kipper trying to make my life hell, Dad hasn't always been the most reliable of dads but, when it came to it, he proved blood *is* thicker than water. When The Kipper showed her true colours, Dad stuck up for his kids and sent her packing.

'I'm not going to put up with some woman screaming like a banshee at me,' Dad says. 'Nag, nag, nag, nag, nag. It went on for *hours*.'

'What?' I'm on to the seafood and pink sauce and almost choke on a prawn. 'You didn't split up because she hated me and Jack?'

'Oh no,' Dad says airily. 'We'd have got round that.' He takes a sip of coffee. 'If I'd known how she felt about you I'd have kept everyone apart. You were probably just a reminder that I had a previous life with your mother. Talking of which, how is she? Still with that ex-army AA guy? Any sign of him moving in or them getting married?'

'Fine, yes, no and no,' I snap, grabbing a sandwich and biting down on it so hard my teeth clatter together.

Oh, gross!

I've bitten into the sarnie that fell on the floor.

As I spit out the bacteria-infested bread I realize I'm not just nuclear-angry but mega-hurt.

Dad gave Caroline Cole her marching orders not

because she hated his kids, but because a woman dared to shout at him.

When I get home I sit on the bed in the Sty in the Sky, as Mum calls my bedroom in the loft conversion, tip everything out of my Top Shop cheapie and start to transfer everything into The Bag of Beauty. I was going to hold off until I'd got rid of the smoky smell but I can't wait to start parading round with it. The girls at school will be sooo jealous.

As I'm unzipping one of the little pockets inside I come across a note.

It's in The Kipper's handwriting:

Dear Electra,
You won. Here's your prize. Enjoy.
Caroline.

I've won but at what price? I think to myself.

I've only had The Bag of Beauty a few hours and in that time I've made a bet that's freaking me out, learnt my dad hasn't stood up for me after all, eaten a potentially life-threatening sandwich, been angry with him and have a sneaking suspicion that, despite what he says, he's probably lonely. On top of all that, I've spent more time stressing over getting the bag dirty than actually enjoying it.

As I carry on moving stuff from one bag to the other, I think of Dad, alone with his new underwear, piercing the plastic on his ready meal, probably trying to work out how to use the microwave.

I finger Caroline's note as I look at the bag.

I love it and I'll do anything to stop Claudia getting her French-mani'd mitts on it but, right now, getting rid of The Kipper doesn't feel quite like the triumphant victory I thought it would.

Chapter Three

Despite the fact that I hated The Kipper, there were a couple of good things that came out of Dad's relationship with her.

The Bag of Beauty, and the fact that she told me I'd make a good lawyer.

As I fancy sending people to jail for doing dreadful things, or even things that aren't really that dreadful but just annoy me, like letting their dog poop on the street and not picking it up, I don't just need to become a lawyer but a judge, although I'm currently reassessing that particular career choice because I'm not sure I could cope with the well-dodgy-looking wig they have to wear. On the plus side, a wig would solve the problem of bad-hair days.

But in order to become a legal eagle I need a degree, which, as I'm having trouble with even the first year of my GCSEs, might be a problem. I am trying to work harder at school, but my butterfly brain gets distracted sooo easily.

Take this morning.

I'm finding it almost impossible to fire up my neurons and tackle an assignment about *My World*, in French, when my English world consists of worrying over whether I'm about to be cornered by an as-yet-unidentified Shrek Head, whether I'll lose The Bag of Beauty to Tits Out, but mostly if I do get to go out with someone who is kissable whether I'll be for ever branded Stiff Lips like Josh Caldwell.

It's not that I haven't snogged before – of *course* I have – but it was once, at the end of a school disco and on so many levels *definitely* with a frog, *not* a prince.

Said snog was with a random French exchange student called Didier Deville, who clearly hadn't managed to pull anyone else for the last smoochy song of the evening, which would explain why, without any warning or sweet talk, he suddenly grabbed me and completely washed my face in slobber. I remember thinking that I should be enjoying it, doing all the knees-sinking and heavy-breathing stuff you see in *Hollyoaks*, but as he chewed my face off all I could think about was whether his spit was washing my make-up off or, worse, whether his rough tongue was going to knock the scab off a particularly brutal zit that had been hanging around the corner of my mouth for weeks (mostly because I kept picking it). In such circumstances I would happily have traded the Spit Spreader for Stiff Lips, as at least Stiff Lips would have been more precise and left my make-up and scab intact.

The unfortunate snog with the Snogging Frog has left me freaked that, should the opportunity to pucker up arise again, I will be drenched in spit or, worse, branded a crap kisser by the other party who might think it's *me* that's doing all the spit-spreading, completely oblivious to the fact that all the gurgling and sucking noises are coming from *him*.

Me and the girls used to spend hours working on the Snogability Scale, rating boys from one (not so much snogging as mouth-to-mouth resuscitation), to five (snogging a Lurve God), and lots of scores in between. This was purely based on how snogable a boy *looked*, but didn't take into account the quality of the snog itself, which thinking about it now, makes the scoring system useless. As Josh Caldwell shows, you can look lush but still be a rubbish smoocher.

It's time to plan a new snogging scale, one based on snogging technique and expert use of the lips rather than just how cute a lad looks. I ignore my French and start doodling, drawing lips, open, closed and some looking downright weird as if they have a huge weeping cold sore on them.

At the bottom of the scale would be a Spit Spreader, a boy who leaves your entire face sopping wet, possibly exfoliating your skin with his tongue.

In other words, Didier Deville.

And now I'm stuck.

Tragically, only a bottom-of-the-rung Spit Spreader has ever kissed me. It's going to take all my imagination to come up with the other categories.

I do more doodling and thinking.

Second from bottom I'd put a Plunge Pucker, the sort of kiss where you're not sure whether they're kissing you or sucking the inside of your mouth out. I've seen snogs like that on telly, and it always reminds me of my dad's firm, Plunge It Plumbing Services, as they're in the business of unblocking loos and drains.

Thirdly, I'd put Stiff Lips. Rigid lips aren't good, but must be better than being subjected to a Spit Spreader or Plunge Pucker snog, plus I know Stiff Lip snogs exist because Claudia and Josh Caldwell had one.

A good kiss is probably a boy with Soft Lips, not knee-trembling, just a nice smoochy snog with flexible lips, hardly any spit and no plunging. I sit back for a moment and think what would be the best type of snog, the top of the pile, the sort of mind-blowing snog you'd want to both carry on for ever, but pause just for a moment so you can text the girls to let them know what's happening.

That's got to be a Lush Lips snog, with fireworks going off in the background. The sort of snog I used to imagine I'd have with Jags.

I think about the bag bet.

Even though Jags isn't quite the Lurve God I thought he was, it does seem a shame to waste all those hours I spent imagining snogging him not to try out the real thing if I'm handed the opportunity on a plate.

My mind conjures up a picture of Jags sitting on a plate, and I'm rather alarmed to find that instead of a tasty Spaniard on there, I wish it was a four-cheese pizza. What is *wrong* with me?

But let's just say that I get a date with Jags, even if it's only because Claudia forces him into it, and a miracle happens and I am on the verge of having a Spanish Snog. What if I got it all wrong? Bumped faces, chewed his nose by mistake or just plain couldn't do it? The opportunity for further snogging practice with him would be lost and, worse, I'd have such a terrible kissing reputation I'd be stuck dating Spit Spreaders for ever.

What would be really useful is if you could snog

yourself in the privacy of your own bedroom so you had an idea of whether you were doing it right, and if not, what you were doing wrong, and then you could practise on yourself until you were snog perfect. I mean, it's ridiculous! David Beckham didn't just grab a ball one day and go straight out and play for England, did he? He spent *years* practising before he got picked for the team. He was at it *constantly*! Without practice, how am I expected to launch myself on to the world stage of kissing, i.e. an actual date with a proper person – not a desperate exchange student in the dark – and deliver a kiss that is perfect in length, lip softness and moisture level? Josh Caldwell probably only had stiff lips because he was out of practice, which was why he was snogging Claudia.

But I've got no one to practise on.

Somehow I need to snog myself and see person-to-person just how much spit I spread and over what area. If I turn out to be a Spit Spreader myself, then I will have to practise reducing my saliva output; though I have no idea how you dampen down your salivary glands as, annoyingly, that doesn't seem to be on the GCSE biology syllabus.

Then I have it.

My full-length mirror on the inside of the wardrobe door!

I hardly ever look at my whole body because I prefer to take my bod segment-by-dodgy-segment, but, for now, the mirror is perfect. Not only can I snog myself, by looking at saliva smeared on the mirror, I will be able to see both amount and spread of spit. I know I'm supposed to be doing French homework and biology is next, but this is a sort of scientific experiment, though not one I'm likely to hand in as part of my homework.

I open the wardrobe door, kick the clothes that have fallen out to one side, try not to focus on my enormous forehead, and with a fluttering tummy and hammering heart, slowly move towards my face.

But then I stop.

Should I keep my eyes open or closed? If I was snogging a lad, I think I'd keep my eyes closed unless I was on the lookout for a better snogging partner. But as there's no way a Lurve God is going to walk through my bedroom door I'll keep them closed. Seeing my own reflection would be well weird.

Here goes . . .

'What are you doing?'

'YEOW!' I've just slammed my face into the mirror with the shock of being caught about to snog myself by The Little Runt.

I spin round to see him standing in my room,

convulsed with giggles.

'You stupid little scroat!' I scream. He knows he's dead meat if he comes into my room unannounced so he'd better start enjoying his final moments. 'Look what you've done!'

My nose is throbbing, although when I peer into the mirror there doesn't seem to be any blood running down my face, which is mega-disappointing as that would *really* get him into trouble with Mum.

'What were you doing?' Jack asks, still giggling. 'Why was your face so close to the mirror?'

'I walked into the door,' I snap. 'What did you think I was doing?'

Jack starts sniggering behind his hand. 'I saw you. I think you were lady kissing. I think you were going to *mwah mwah* yourself.' He pretends to lick the palm of his hand. I'll show his face the palm of my hand if he doesn't shut up.

'GET OUT OF MY ROOM, SCROAT FACE!' I yell, chucking the nearest thing I can find at him, which, unfortunately, is The Bag of Beauty.

It hits him square in the chest, padlock first, and then falls to the ground where everything including Tampax and an unwrapped panty-liner falls out.

The Little Runt makes a great fuss and staggers around

pretending he can't breathe, although lack of breath doesn't stop him yelling at the top of his voice, 'I CAN'T BREATHE! I CAN'T BREATHE!' over and over again.

I hear two sets of footsteps hurtling up three sets of stairs towards the attic, so it's only moments before Mum and Phil are in my room.

'What's wrong, love?' Mum sounds alarmed. She bends down to a sobbing Jack who's now rolling on the floor, clutching his chest. 'Why can't you breathe?'

'Has he swallowed something?' Phil says. 'Or stuck something up his nose again?'

'Poo Head hit me,' he sobs. 'I think my chest is broken.'

Phil stands in the doorway as Mum pulls Jack's jumper up. There's a bright-red mark on his pale scrawny body.

'She threw her bag at me on purpose and a metal thingy hit me.' There's lots of sobbing and snotting going on. 'She tried to kill me.'

Ooh, he's making a meal of it. Some nine-year-olds would be grateful that if they *had* to be hit by something, it was designer leather and brass.

'Did you?' Mum asks, knowing that whilst it's perfectly likely that I *have* tried to kill my brother, it's also perfectly likely that it could be a genuine accident and that The Little Runt is playing up.

'Yes,' I say defiantly.

'Why?' Phil asks.

'Because the Snivelling Grub annoyed me,' I say in a tone of voice that I hope conveys Phil's asked a ridiculous question. 'He came into my room without asking.'

'We'd been calling and calling you for lunch,' Mum says sharply. 'I sent Jack up to get you. What were you doing that you didn't hear us? And what's wrong with your nose? It looks red.'

'She was lady kissing,' Jack says. 'I saw her.'

'He's a mentalist!' I snap, glaring at The Little Runt. 'I walked into my wardrobe mirror because I tripped over a pile of clothes.'

'It's hardly surprising, your room's such a tip,' Mum says, hauling a still-sobbing Jack to his feet. She picks up The Bag of Beauty. 'When did you get this? Is it a fake?'

'No,' I say as The Little Runt bends down, picks up the naked panty-liner and wipes his nose with it. I wouldn't mind if it was just me and Mum here, but Phil's standing in the door and, despite the fact he's practically living here, he's not officially family, and you don't want non-official family members to see your sanitary supplies being used inappropriately. 'I told you. That was the parcel I got yesterday. Caroline Cole sent me the bag.'

From downstairs comes a terrible wailing and screeching.

The smoke alarm.

'Oh no!' Mum shrieks.

She rushes out, followed by Phil and the moments-earlier-dying Jack.

The smoke alarm is silenced, I can hear pots and pans being rattled in the basement kitchen, and Phil hollers 'Electra, ready!' up the stairs.

I look in the mirror and think for a moment.

Mum and Phil are busy.

Jack won't come back into my room, not because he knows I'd kill him, but because there'll soon be roasties, meat and gravy on the kitchen table.

I'm on my own.

I'm going to have a quick Spanish Snog.

The reflection in the mirror isn't a wide-faced teen with mottled salami limbs, lank mousy hair and a getting-redder-by-the-minute nose. It's a Spanish Lurve God with liquid-brown come-snog-me eyes and dark, slightly wavy hair. He's forgotten all about the other girls he's snogged, even Claudia Barnes. It's only me he's ever wanted. He's just been waiting for the right moment.

I lean in.

My heart's beating faster.

I close my eyes.

My breathing's getting heavier.

My lips touch the mirror and . . .

I jump back with horror, not because Jack's come back in the room, or I'm freaked at what I'm doing, or even the fact that when my nose touched the cold glass I realized it *really* hurt.

No, the reason I jumped back is because I intended to kiss Javier Antonio Garcia, but he turned into Frazer Burns.

And as I rub my throbbing beak I realize I've got my Plan B.

Plan B is Plan Burns.

I'm going to get Frazer Burns to ask me out.

Chapter Four

'I'm just going out,' I shout down from the hall. 'I won't be long.'

'Electra, it's eight o'clock!' Mum shouts back. 'It's way too late to go out now!'

'I need a walk!' I shriek. 'I've been cooped up doing homework all day!'

Not strictly true if you count the time I spent snogging myself and working out the new snogging scale, *and* the fact I had to rewrite most of my French homework. When I looked at it after lunch, in amongst all the *ouis, nons* and *maintenants* I'd doodled loads of hearts and lips and made notes on the new kissing categories. I know that the French are supposed to be a nation of lovers but, out of context and written in black biro in a school exercise book, the words *spit, pucker* and *stiff* didn't seem very romantic.

'Electra, come down for a moment.'

Hmm. This could be a problem. My *Just going out for a walk* cover is going to be blown apart, unless it's usual to go for a walk dressed like a teenage tart at eight o'clock on a Sunday evening. And of course, I'm not *really* going *just* for a walk. I'm going to go round to FB's on the cunning pretext of wanting him to check my maths homework, when really it's to get him to ask me out and get one step ahead of Claudia and her cunning Plan C.

I'm still formulating Plan B, but I'm thinking about dropping mega-hints about having nothing to do on Friday night accompanied by lots of heavy sighing, and hope he suggests we do nothing on Friday night together and that there is torrential rain so that he looks lush. Perhaps I should check the long-range weather forecast first and choose the day of the week I mention by how wet it's likely to be.

I didn't mean to look tarty. My plan had been to be quite careful with my Frazer-baiting outfit as I didn't want him to be frightened of the whole push-up bra, low-top, wobbling-cleavage, high-heels and bumster-jeans approach that Claudia Barnes takes, so I toned it down to just The Bag of Beauty, a push-up bra on its tightest hook and lots of lip gloss, no coat, but jeans *obviously*. Even for a Lush Lipper I wouldn't go out on a cold November night in just my knickers. Then I started wondering whether even if I threw myself at his feet with a sticker on my forehead saying *Ask me out, please!* FB would get the hint, so at the last minute I panicked, put heels on, stuffed a couple of socks in my bra and fluffed up my hair.

I think boys will like this look, but I doubt my mother will.

I go downstairs where Phil and Mum are slumped on the sofa watching telly.

Mum swivels her head round.

'How's your face?' she asks. 'Still sore?'

'Fine,' I say, which isn't true, but if I tell Mum my nose is throbbing, I've got a bit of a headache and, worryingly, the skin under my eyes seems to be looking weirdly dark, she'll defo stop me from streetwalking.

'You've got my coat on.' Mum pulls a face. 'Why?'

To put her off the boy-baiting scent I'd left my tarts' trotters by the front door, dumped the bling bag in the hall and grabbed Mum's coat from the end of the stairs as a cover-up for the slightly tarty outfit, although even in the privacy of my own home I'm deeply freaked to find my body clad in a vast red nylon anorak, not just an anorak, but one with a hood with a white fake-fur trim and silver plastic toggles.

On second thoughts, as he's geeky, FB might go for the dorky prostitute look.

'It's cold,' I say, wrapping the coat around me. 'And I'm only going round the block.'

'And you needed half a tube of lip gloss to be able to walk?'

Clearly Mum isn't as daft as I sometimes hope she is.

I give a heavy sigh accompanied by an eye roll. 'OK, I'm going round to Frazer Burns's house so he can help me with my maths homework.'

'You said you'd done your homework,' Phil pipes up, which mega-irritates me because I don't think non-parentals should interfere in my academic timetable.

'I have,' I say, which is partly true. I've done maths and French, but I'm not going to mention there's still business studies to start and last week's history to finish.

'So, why do you need help?' he asks.

'Oh for goodness' . . .' I stop myself snapping at Phil, as then Mum will ground me for the night. 'I've spent hours fiddling around with fractions and I want to make sure I've got the right answers. What's the point of slaving over a hot calculator if you then get crappy marks?'

Phil seems convinced and turns back to the telly, but Mum still stares at me.

'Is Frazer Burns your boyfriend?' she says, giving me one of her best Suspicious Mother looks. 'Or are you hoping he will be?'

45

'Oh gross!' I shriek. 'You've seen him. He's a terminally uncool freak boy! And do you think I'd be going out dressed in this dorky coat if I wanted some lad to ask me out!'

'I like your mum in that coat,' Phil says over his shoulder. 'Especially with the hood up.'

Mum gives me a final suspicious stare.

'I want you and my coat back by nine,' she says. 'Not one second later. OK?'

Before I go up the drive of 7 Compton Avenue I take the dorky anorak off, sling it over my arm, push up the push-up bra, fluff my hair up a bit more and lick my lips, which is actually a stupid thing to do as I seem to have swallowed most of my carefully applied Rose Sugar lip gloss. Then, under a blaze of security lights, I crunch confidently up the drive. Not an easy thing to do in spindly heels.

I ring the bell.

Archie Dog goes mental from somewhere in the house, but doesn't come flying to the door as he usually does.

There's a hall light on, lots of dog barking but no sign of anyone.

I try the bell again.

Still no sign of human activity.

This is a disaster! I was sure FB would be in. He's always in. Who other than someone like me goes out on a Sunday night?

I walk back to the gate and decide to hang around for a bit in case the family Burns come back. But if I hang around, does it look desperate? I mean, I *am* desperate but I don't want to look as if I am. I want to look casual, as if I've either just arrived or am just leaving.

I totter back up the drive, ring the bell, wait for a moment as the dog barks and no one comes, walk back down the drive and out into the street.

Then it's back up the drive, another ring of the bell and so on.

This is good! It's a nice little routine and doesn't look as if I'm lying in wait, just as if I called round at the precise moment FB and his family arrived home. Another benefit is it keeps my feet moving as if I stand still for too long I'll get frostbite in my toes. Silver sandals outside in winter are only good if you're tottering from car to house or bus to shop, not streetwalking.

I don't know how many up-and-down-the-drive marches I've done, but I'm back at the gate and about to turn for another go when a man jumps out of the bushes and I scream.

In a nanosecond the following train of thought runs

through my head: *Oh no! I'm going to be attacked, possibly murdered! Double Oh no! Newspaper reports will describe me carrying this dorky anorak, something I could never live down, even if I was dead. I'd rather be dead than a dork!*

And then I think, *How come I'm having a fashion crisis when I'm about to be murdered?*

I can be *very* shallow.

'Ernest Ferguson. Compton Avenue Neighbourhood Watch Coordinator. What are you up to?'

In the gloomy street my attacker looks so old he could be dead, though I expect the dead don't wear glasses and a tweed flat cap.

'You could have given me a heart attack jumping out like that!' I shriek. 'I thought you were a perve!'

Of course, just because he hasn't groped me yet doesn't mean he isn't. There's still time for him to drag me into the bushes.

'My wife and I have been watching you,' he says, peering at me through his thick lenses. 'You've been up and down that drive fourteen times, beginning at seventeen minutes past eight.'

'So?' I say. 'There's no law against it, is there?'

'Depends on your motives,' Almost Dead says. 'Depends on *why* you're marching up and down private property.'

'I'm waiting for the family that lives there to come

home,' I say. 'I was walking up and down to keep warm.'

'You could always try putting your coat on,' Almost Dead snaps. 'You're upsetting the dog, that's why he keeps barking. Enid and I were watching *Midsomer Murders* but we heard the commotion. Good burglar alarms, dogs.'

'I'm sorry about the dog,' I say, deciding that I'm so cold I'm going to ditch any attempt at style and put Mum's coat back on. 'Do you know when they're going to be back?'

Almost Dead snorts. 'First rule of defence. Never give away valuable information to the enemy. You could be part of a burglary ring and feed information back to your accomplices.'

'What accomplices?' I say. The man might not be a perve, but he's definitely a mentalist. I thought our neighbours, the Snooping Skinners, were professional curtain twitchers, but they're amateurs compared to this weirdo.

'Those.'

He nods towards the Avenue where Pinhead, Gibbo and Spud have started hurtling up and down the centre of the road on skateboards. Well, Gibbo and Spud are hurtling. Pinhead seems to be having trouble staying on his board, probably because by the looks of it he's got a can in one hand and a cigarette in the other.

'I've got a good mind to call the police,' Almost Dead says.

I've had enough.

I'm out of here.

Even with the dorky coat I'm as cold as Jack Frost, I've no Plan B date, homework to start and finish, I'm being interrogated by a mentalist, and my bra strap is so tight it's practically cutting my chest in two.

'I'm off,' I tell Almost Dead, sticking my hood up and stomping off as quickly as I can in unsuitable footwear.

'Who shall I say called?' he shouts after me.

'Jack Frost!' I yell back.

I'm halfway down Compton Avenue, picking my way through dog mess and uneven paving stones, when a skateboard skids to a halt in front of me, and I look up to see Pinhead, Gibbo and Spud blocking the pavement. Pinhead is doing his teen Grim Reaper impression, his grey hood framing his sunken face, his shoulders hunched and his bony arms sticking out the end of his hoodie. The other two just look like a couple of chavvy oiks.

I wonder if wearing my mum's anorak hood up automatically makes me a hoodie.

'So, what's it going to be, boys? Shag, marry or push off a cliff?' Pinhead taunts, blowing fag smoke into the air.

'Get lost,' I snap, trying to get past, but not wanting to bump into them and contaminate The Bag of Beauty or, worse, brush against Pinhead's lit ciggy. Dirt I could clean, but a fag burn would be *fatal* to posh leather.

'I'd say, shag and *then* push off a cliff.'

Spud and Gibbo snort, and I make a mental note to lure all three of them to the highest cliff I can think of and push *them* off, perhaps on our geography field trip next year. That should make writing up my notes more interesting.

'No wonder they call you Pinhead,' I sneer. 'A head and a brain the size of a pin. And if your head and your brain is small, the rest of you probably is too!' I nod in the general direction of Pinhead's bits, without actually looking there.

Spud and Gibbo snigger behind their hands.

Pinhead steps forward, and even though he's about a foot taller than me I can smell tobacco and cheap booze on his breath. I tuck The Bag of Beauty inside Mum's anorak just in case Pinhead is so drunk he voms cider over it. No amount of airing in the garden and Febreze would get rid of *that* smell.

'Like you'd ever find out, Lekky,' he leers. 'We all think you're a lezzer, but maybe you're not 'cause you're always sniffing around The Beakster's place.'

'I'd rather be a lezzer than go out with a rat-faced slug like you!' I say.

'Oooh!' they all jeer.

'Let me past or, or . . .' I don't know what to say, so I twirl the plastic toggles in what I hope is a threatening manner. Ideally, I'd like to swipe them with The Bag of Beauty's brass padlock, but I don't want designer goods involved in a street fight.

'So, how far have you got with The Beakster?' Pinhead sneers. 'First base, second, or can The Beakster go *all* the way with you?'

The three oiks are laughing and snorting and sniggering.

'Oh shut up and leave me alone, amoeba brain,' I snap, kicking the skateboard out of the way.

I kick it harder than I intended, and it rolls out into the road and in front of a police car coming slowly up Compton Avenue.

The car swerves to miss it, but in doing so mounts the pavement.

Then it stops, two policemen get out and, as I stand there nervously twiddling my toggles, wondering what to do next, The Grim Reaper and his gang leg it into the darkness.

Chapter Five

Mum was quite relaxed about my run-in with the police.

I told her as soon as I got home and she agreed none of it was my fault, I was just in the wrong place at the wrong time but, as it turned out, wearing the right coat for two reasons.

Firstly, I got the impression the police couldn't possibly believe a teenager in a shapeless red anorak with a fake-fur trim would be the sort to get in trouble, so they totally believed me when I said the oiks had blocked the pavement and I'd only kicked the skateboard to try and get away.

And secondly, as I was talking to the police, the Burnses' dark-blue BMW came up the street and in my hoodie disguise I doubt anyone recognized me.

The police asked for the names of the lads that legged it, though I had to think really hard to remember their proper names, rather than their nicknames.

When I said, 'Stephen Prescott' (which is Pinhead's real name), one of the policemen said, 'Ah,' in a very knowing way, and told me to steer clear of all of them in future. Which I would, if I could, but it's quite difficult if they're always hanging around the streets and are in some of my classes at school.

But Mum isn't relaxed this morning.

She's standing outside my bedroom door yelling, 'Electra! If you don't come out of your room at once, I'm coming in!'

It's gone eight and I should be at the bus stop by now, but I stay sitting on the end of my bed, still in my PJs.

'Electra!' I can tell by the sharp tone of her voice she's just about ready to storm my bedroom, battering down the door with her Mighty Mammaries, which seem to have got even mightier recently.

'I've told you, I'm not going to school looking like this!' I yell back.

'What crisis is it this time?' Mum shouts. 'A spot? A bad-hair day? A broken fingernail? What?'

She's not going to give up, so I swing my legs off the end of the bed, pad in bare feet across the laminate floor and open the door.

'Happy now?' I say accusingly.

'Oh, love!'

Mum's attitude has instantly changed from Suspicious Mum to Concerned Mum as she inspects my two black eyes. I look like a raccoon with a swollen nose and zits.

'They must have come up in the night,' I moan. Even thick yellow Butterface-style make-up won't cover these shiners. 'I think my eyes might fall out of their sockets.'

'We'd better get someone to take a look at you,' Mum says, tipping my head back and staring at me. 'I'll take Jack to school and then come back and get you. Put your uniform on so you can go straight in afterwards.'

Bummer!

I was hoping two black eyes would mean a day off, but as Mum isn't medically qualified, perhaps the doc will have a different view and write me a sick note.

Mum heads off to round up The Little Runt and run him to Hilmartin Junior School, and I text the girls to say I'm going to be late because I've had a fight with a wardrobe door, extricate my tartan kilt, green jumper and green blazer from under a pile of clothes on the back of a chair, and fish out one of the newly ironed white shirts Mum has put in my wardrobe over the weekend.

No one's going to ask me out looking like a raccoon, not even FB or the most desperate Shrek Head, I think to myself as I loop the green polyester noose around my neck and make a thick low knot. Still, I never really wanted a date with Jags in the first place, and it means I get to keep The Bag of Beauty.

I look at it sitting on top of my chest of drawers. There's no *way* Claudia Barnes is going to get her mitts on my Chloé.

I'm never going to give that bag up. *Ever*.

'Back already, Mrs Brown. Is everything all right?' a prim-looking receptionist enquires as Mum walks up to the front desk.

'It's my daughter,' Mum nods towards me. 'I'd just like one of the doctors, preferably Dr Chaudhri, to take a look at her. She's had a bit of an accident.'

The receptionist fixes her beady eyes on me and gives an *Are you sure you're ill enough to have one of our precious emergency appointments?* stare, so I lift the pair of enormous bug-eyed sunnies I'm wearing and lean towards her, giving her the full-on double-shiner treatment.

'Oh. I see,' she says, though frankly with these couple of black beauties she'd have to be registered blind not to notice. 'There'll be a wait as Dr Chaudhri is running about twenty minutes late. Take a seat.'

We sit surrounded by people coughing and wheezing and generally looking so unwell I'm beginning to wish I'd gone to school and taken the chance of empty eye sockets. Knowing my luck, I've come here with a couple of bog-standard black eyes and I'll leave with some tropical life-threatening disease. Still, a few weeks in a hospital isolation unit would solve the bag bet problem as even if a cute doctor asked me out Claudia would never get to hear about it, and I rather fancy a couple of weeks snuggled up in bed watching telly and reading magazines.

'Have you been here recently?' I ask Mum as I leaf through a copy of *Hello!* that is so out of date, the celeb wedding on the front has already ended in divorce. 'Reception woman seemed to know you.'

Mum shrugs as Doc Chaudhri comes into the corridor, calls out, 'Mrs Kamara!' and a woman with elephant legs, wearing slippers, shuffles towards an open door.

A girl comes into the surgery so pregnant, her stomach looks like a balloon ready to pop. When I've stopped staring at her sticky-out belly button, which I can't help but notice, not just because of its size or the fact she's wearing a tiny black zip-up top and low-slung grey tracky bottoms, but because she's got an inky-blue sun tattooed around it, I realize it's one of the girls in Year 11, Cassie Taylor I think she's called. She used to hold the school record for the fastest hundred-metre hurdles, but she's obviously not going to be jumping over anything for a while.

She waddles towards the waiting room and heaves herself into a chair next to me.

'All right?' she asks, nodding.

I don't know if she recognizes me or just the minging school uniform.

'Yeah,' I nod back. I'm hoping that the bug-eyed sunnies are disguising the fact that I'm totally horrified that interspersed with the tattooed sunrays around her belly button are deep red stretch marks. The overall effect is one of an explosion across her drum-tight swollen tum.

'When you due?' Cassie asks, rolling gum around her tongue.

'I'm not!' I gasp, sitting up straight in my chair, sucking my gut in and making a mental note that the muffin top *has* to go. 'I've got black eyes.' I raise the sunnies as proof that I'm not preggers.

'Nice one!' she says. 'Who decked you?'

'No one!' I wonder if I really do look like a pregnant schoolgirl who's been in a fight. 'I walked into a door.'

'That's what my mum always used to say when my dad beat her up,' Cassie shrugs. 'Till the cops got 'im for decking my Uncle Gary.'

Elephant Woman shuffles back to reception clutching a

piece of paper, and more patients are called, but not me. As Mum has her head in a copy of *Mother & Baby*, it seems as if I'm stuck with Cassie – and she's the one who should be reading about nappy rash and follow-on milk.

'When's your baby due?' I ask, thinking that at least if Cassie goes into labour here she's in the right place, and I'm not going to be summoned to provide hot water and towels whilst trying to think back to an episode of *Holby City* to remember what to do next.

''Bout two weeks,' she says.

'Who's the dad?'

Cassie shrugs. 'Either Bozza Slater or Macca Gribben. We'll have a test, maybes on TV, and then whichever one it is, I'll get engaged. I've picked what ring I want already. Blinging it is.'

It seems weird that there's only a school year between us and yet I'm here because I was pretending to kiss and had an accident, and she's here because she did kiss and had a different sort of accident.

Mum elbows me, points to the loo and heads towards it. I'm left with Cassie The Pram Face on my own.

'Any thoughts on names?' I ask.

'Yeah,' Cassie smiles, fiddling with one of her selection of earrings and sounding enthusiastic for the first time. 'I know it's a little girl so I'm going to call her Tequila-Becks, you know, after what got me plastered and pregnant. Lovely, isn't it?'

NO, IT IS NOT LOVELY! I want to scream. IT IS AN ABOMINATION THAT POOR CHILD WILL HAVE TO LIVE WITH FOR EVER!

I am *horrified*, not just for me, but for poor Tequila-Becks Taylor/Slater/Gribben whatever her surname ends up being. Parents shouldn't use a theme for naming their children whether it's after herbs like Sorrel's mum (Jasmine, Sorrel, Senna, Basil and Orris), what you were drinking (Tequila-Becks), or where your parents stayed on holiday (me).

I know what it's like to have an odd name. Electra is fine if you're a dark-eyed Greek goddess or a porn star, but totally inappropriate if you're *so* not a glamour puss or Greek girl, and not if the name was chosen purely because your parents spent their Christmas honeymoon in the Electra Self Catering Apartments in Faliraki, Greece, whilst expecting me. But then Mum was only eighteen when she had me, and Cassie is fifteen, maybe sixteen at most, so perhaps if you get pregnant when you're a teenager you're drawn to naff names.

I'm desperate to ask Cassie what she would have called the baby if it had been a boy – Jack Daniels maybe – but as Mum comes back from the loo Dr Chaudhri puts his head into the corridor, bellows, 'Electra Brown?' and I leave Cassie beached in her chair, flicking through an old copy of *heat* magazine.

Chapter Six

'So, you like, just walked into a door?' Tam asks.

I'm at school, having lunch, as Mum forced me to go in, even driving me to the school and waiting until I'd gone through the gates.

Annoyingly, Doc Chaudhri said my eyes had only minor bruising, which will fade over the next couple of weeks, and that unless I started having headaches and/or dizzy spells, I was fine to go to school and get on with *normal life*. I'm not sure what the medical profession thinks is normal, but I can tell you that whacking yourself in the face whilst trying to snog yourself in the mirror doesn't sound normal to me, but I guess if I'd told the doc how I got the black eyes, he'd have whipped me off to the sort of funny farm Tamara's dad found himself in when he had his nervous breakdown.

'Were you drunk?' Claudia asks, as if I'm likely to be plastered in my room on a Sunday lunchtime.

'Yeah, right!' I laugh. 'But talking of drunk, when I was at the doc's this morning I saw that girl in Year 11 who's preggers, Cassie Taylor. Due in two weeks and about to burst. Anyway, she's expecting a girl and she's going to call it Tequila-Becks!'

'Oh cute!' Claudia coos as Luce giggles, and Sorrel splutters her apple juice over the table.

'Classy, making it a double name,' Butterface says seriously.

Tamara Lennox-Hill keeps quiet. I expect coming from a posh background and with an older brother called Rupert at boarding school, she's well aware that Tequila-Becks is neither classy nor cute, but she's not going to say it. Until halfway through Year 9 she was at Queen Beatrice's School for Snotty-Nosed Girls, but after her dad's breakdown, Mr Lennox-Hill lost his job, Rupe stayed at boarding school and Tam was thrown to the chavs (her old friends from QB's words, not mine), and is stuck at Burke's for her GCSEs.

'Who's the father?' Claudia asks, pushing her tray away, leaning back over her chair and sticking her boobs out. 'I heard it was Bozza Slater, you know, the one who works at the Esso garage behind the till.'

'She says it's him or Macca Gribben,' I say, having no idea who either of these lads are.

'Well, *he's* not going to be there at the birth.' Tits Out pulls a face. 'He's on remand for the arson attack on the bus garage.'

At the far end of the hall, FB is sitting on his own at a table, eating a sandwich, bent over a yellow Tupperware box. He looks lonely and a bit lost. Maybe I'm only having weirdly inappropriate thoughts about him because I feel sorry for him. Perhaps dating him would be like charity work, services to the unfortunate and all that. That's probably it, I want to pity snog him. But then why can't *I* get pity snogs or pity dates? Perhaps *I'd* look better soaking wet the way FB does.

'You with us?' Claudia kicks me gently in the shins.

'Oh, soz.' I stop staring at FB and wondering whether a session down the slides at Aqua Splash would, in fact, be our perfect date, as not only would we *both* be wet, I could blame the slides on flattening out my thighs and making them look meatier than they actually are, *and* grab a slice of pizza in the pool-side café afterwards. 'What were you saying?'

'I was just asking if anyone had asked you out yet, but you've obviously got someone in mind to help you win the bet and lose me the fab bag,' Claudia giggles.

I arrange my face into what I hope is a *What are you talking about?* look.

'You were looking all dreamy in Razor Burns's direction,' Claudia prompts. 'We saw you.'

'Him?' I squeak. 'Freak Boy? Get lost, Claudia! I'd rather you had the bag than go out with *him*.'

As I say this, I feel *terrible* that I've been so jelly-spined and shallow. I should have stuck up for FB, told the truth, admitted I have racy thoughts about him featuring water and pizza, and that I probably *was* looking dreamily in his direction. But if I had fessed up, could I have coped with the girls teasing and trying to humiliate me?

'I don't think he's like, that freaky any longer,' Tam says, clearly not worrying about such things herself. 'If you look at him now, he looks, well, like, different. And he's loads taller this term.'

'Perhaps he's had a facelift,' Nat says. 'Or his nose fixed. I saw a prog about men having stuff like that done. They can even get their bits made longer.'

'I've always liked him,' Lucy says, changing the weird-surgery subject. 'He's got a lovely personality.'

'Who cares about that?' Claudia says. 'I don't know what it is, but he's defo different. Maybe his face is getting bigger so his nose looks smaller. Must be his raging hormones. Makes everything bigger!'

Everyone but Sorrel and me collapses in fits of giggles. I'm not giggling because I can't bear to think of what Claudia's suggesting, and Sorrel's not giggling because since the Warren thing, well, she hardly ever laughs.

'I think he's, like, quite cute, in a like, sort of odd way,' Tam says, staring at him putting the lid back on his lunchbox.

'You gave him a minger score only a few months ago,' I remind her, feeling weird that someone other than me is starting to see FB in a different light. 'You said he was top male minger at Burke's.'

'Well, I'm like, changing my mind,' Tam says. 'Frazer Burns defo has *potential*.'

I am truly freaked at the thought of Tammy Two-Names fancying FB. Not only is she prettier than me, she's brighter than me and much *much* posher. She'd easily fit into the Burnses' granite kitchen and swish conservatory life.

But if I fancy him and Tam fancies him, there could be other, as yet unknown threats to Plan B.

What if he becomes the Burke's equivalent of Jags, not Spanish, or short, or even dark and swarthy, but lusted after?

What if all the QB girls start fancying him, not just ex-Queen Bees like Tam? People at different schools are always more fanciable (within reason; I doubt anyone would ever fancy Pinhead, Gibbo and Spud) and if girls like Fritha Kennedy and her bitchy glossy clan start targeting FB and tossing their hair in his direction I'll never get a look-in.

'What about you, Sorrel?' Tits Out asks. 'Where do you stand on the *Is Frazer Burns a god or a geek* debate?'

'He's still a freakin' weirdo,' Sorrel snarls.

I'm on my own after school, not great when you're facing a double-stress situation and have no one to freak out with. Bella picked Luce up, Sorrel has the dentist *again*, I can't talk to Claudia because she's probably working on Plan C right now, I never discuss serious stuff with Nat and Tam's off limits because she's now The Enemy, about to scupper my Plan Burns by swiping FB from under my nose. This isn't just because he's more likely to fancy some posh totty, even one with braces, but because Tamara Lennox-Hill is the sort of girl who might pin him against the bus stop and snog him, whereas I'd wait to be asked first.

What am I going to do?

I'm so seriously stressed I need emergency chocolate, so decide to make a detour to the newsagent's near home. It's drizzling and I know what I said about the muffin top going, but this isn't the time to start stinting on the carbs, not when there's so many traumas in my life.

I go in, grab a Snickers bar, hand over the money to Mr Patel and between getting my change and leaving the shop, I've already ripped open the chocolate log, taken a bite and am starting on munch number two.

That's how stressed I am.

I'm just fishing a bit of toffee-coated peanut from between my teeth with my bus pass when I see FB heading towards me. He must have got home already, one of the advantages of cycling to school, although he's still in his uniform. When he sees me he stops for a moment and I think he's going to do the normal thing boys do when they see me, i.e. run away, but amazingly he carries on walking towards me.

'Hi!' FB says shyly. As he's only slightly drizzle-damp rather than rain-soaked sopping, I'd say he was warm on the looks front rather than hot. 'I'm just going to buy a magazine.'

He hovers for a moment, and I'd like to say something but my mouth is full of toffee, chocolate and peanuts. By the time I've unglued my gnashers of gooey confectionery, FB's disappeared into the shop.

Damn! I've missed my chance to get to him before Tam does. She wouldn't have waited for her teeth to be clean!

She'd snog him on the pretext of needing his tongue to fish the nuts and toffee out of her molars.

I need to act quickly. Follow him in on the pretence of buying something. Put Plan B straight into action. Pretend to be bored on Friday night and hope he takes the hint.

Here goes.

My arrival in the shop is announced by a buzzer which sounds like an angry wasp trapped in a jar. Still, at least FB knows I'm here. He's standing by the computer section, flicking through a magazine.

'Hi,' he says again, half smiling.

'Hi,' I say, half smiling as well, not because I'm half happy to see him or being all coy, but because I'm wondering if my teeth are clean or stuffed with nut sprinkled toffee.

'I didn't get a chance to say anything at school, but your eyes. What happened?' FB peers into my bruised eyes with his rather lovely green ones.

'I walked into a door,' I say. 'The doc says they should fade soon.'

'Perhaps you should get your eyes checked. I mean, you don't want to keep walking into things. I've read there are nearly a million blind or partially sighted people in England alone.'

I don't know what to say. FB definitely looks less freaky than he used to, but he's still *very* odd the way he recites weird facts and strange numbers.

There's an awkward silence.

He goes back to studying his mag, and I'm a bit miffed to see that he'd rather check out the latest laptops than check out me.

I try to think of something devastatingly witty and computer-related to say, thereby showing him that not only am I interested in geek stuff (a lie) but that I also have a good sense of humour, when FB says, 'I'm glad we bumped into each other, though I didn't mean literally, not like you and the door.'

My heart starts to beat faster, and I try to look as gorgeous as I can, which is probably impossible in school uniform with my jaws clamped shut and drizzle-limp locks.

'Did you come round on Sunday night?'

Time to play it cool. Even if FB does fancy me, I don't want him to think I've spent half an hour marching up and down his drive like some deranged soldier in lip gloss, heels and a padded bra.

'Me? Nah. What made you think that?'

That was good. Very cool. Very casual. Kept my mouth almost closed.

'The man next door said a girl was hanging round our house last night.'

'Well, it wasn't me.' I say this in a *How could you possibly think it was me?* tone which I enforce with a slightly haughty *As if!* half-laugh.

I grab a random mag.

'I didn't think it was. Mr Ferguson said the girl was a bit slutty and was hanging around with three lads who sounded like Pinhead and his lot.'

I knew I looked a *little* tarty but I didn't think I looked that cheap!

'And Dad said there was another girl, an odd one who looked pregnant talking to the police in the road when we got back,' FB says. 'I wonder what that was all about.'

Odd? Slutty? Pregnant? I'm clearly not projecting the sort of image I would like to, though the preggy-belly was the Chloé under the dorky anorak.

There's more silence and FB doesn't seem to be about to fill it, but goes back to his magazine. If he keeps studying it, at this rate he won't need to buy it.

I need to work fast. I can't let this opportunity slip by, not just to win the bet and keep the bag but also to stop Tammy nabbing FB. *I* was the one who saw his potential first. *I* was the one who was having inappropriate thoughts about him long before his face grew or his nose didn't or whatever hormones have done to his body. If anyone deserves a chance with FB, it's *me*.

'This will come in useful on Friday night. Should give me something to do.' I confidently tap the front of the mag I grabbed.

FB glances at it. 'You're making compost on Friday night?'

I look at the mag. Oh no! It's *Gardener's World*. The cover has a compost bin with a Christmas tree stuck in the top.

'Well, Friday nights are so boring,' I say, trying to sound breezy, even though I feel a bit panicky. 'It's just the same old, same old. The girls are always busy and I never know what to do. Friday nights are not just boring they're B.O.R.I . . .' I'm getting flustered now, and why on earth have I started to spell out words? The inappropriate choice of magazine and the whole composting-on-a-Friday-night thing has put me off my planned speech. 'D.'

And wrecked my spelling.

'Borid?' FB sounds as confused as I sound flustered. 'Your Friday nights are – *borid*?'

'No! Yes! I mean I got confused between being boring and horrid,' I say, wondering if Mr Patel will let me grab another Snickers bar and ram it in my mouth before paying for it.

'Well, I find Friday nights borid too!' FB laughs, looking a bit red around his neck.

The wasp starts buzzing and Pinhead saunters in, hood up, head down. He grabs a can of Red Bull from the fridge and bangs it on the counter. Just as I think we've got away without being spotted he drops some money on the floor, and as he bends down to pick it up, he clocks us.

'Well, if it isn't The Beakster and Lekky the lesbo.'

'Ignore him,' I order FB, who *is* ignoring him and continues to read his magazine.

'Love the eyes,' Pinhead taunts. 'The whacked-in-the-face look really does it for me.'

'Oh get lost, you rat,' I snap. 'You're such a slug head!'

'You can't actually be a mammal *and* a gastropod,' FB whispers to me.

'Didn't you get your fix of The Beakster last night?' Pinhead sneers. 'When you were hanging around his house?'

'It *was* you!' FB says, which is a bit of a worry given that I was described as either a pram-face or a slut. 'Why did you come round?'

'She came round for a bit of beaky action!' Pinhead jeers. 'She was sniffing around your place, Beakster!'

'I went for help with my homework,' I say. 'Quadratic equations do my head in!'

'Yeah, right! Some extra-curricular activity!' Pinhead taunts, though frankly I'm amazed he knows what extra-curricular means.

The buzzer goes again and Tits Out totters in. She's still in school uniform, but she's changed into shiny black thigh-length spiky-heeled boots.

'Only three young people at any one time!' Mr Patel shrieks. 'One of you has to go.'

'Come on,' I say to FB. 'Let's *both* go.'

'You two look cosy,' Claudia says, ignoring a leering Pinhead and grabbing a can of Tango. 'What you up to?'

'We were just talking about how boring Friday nights can be,' I say, hoping to shut Claudia up and get out of the way of Pinhead who can't keep his eyes off her plakky-clad thighs. 'Nothing major.'

'No wonder your Fridays are boring if you're hanging around with beaky losers like him,' Pinhead sneers. 'Go out with me and I'll show you how good a Friday night can be.' He looks me up and down which makes my skin crawl.

I'm just about to tell Pinhead that I'd rather spend my Friday nights eating beetle dung on toast than go out with him, when I see Claudia looking smug.

The bet!

Plan A *and* Plan B have failed. This is Plan C.

'Is this down to you?' I hiss at Tits Out, as behind me Mr Patel chants, 'Only three! Only three!'

'Not me,' Claudia says, sounding genuinely disgusted and looking as innocent as a teenage tart can. 'What do you take me for?'

'I'd take you for anything,' Pinhead guffaws.

I stare straight into Claudia's eyes, and after I've wondered how she manages to wear so much mascara without her lashes snapping off, I realize I believe her. Claudia might be many things, but even *she* wouldn't set me up on a date with the leering lanky louse of a school bully.

'So, are you going out with Pinhead or not?' she says, and I know that even if she didn't set me up with Pinhead, a bet's a bet, and she's not going to let me out of this one if it's a chance of owning cream-leather designer bling. The bet was that I wouldn't go out with the next lad to ask me, and that next lad is the teen Grim Reaper.

I sooo don't want to go out with Pinhead.

I no longer care about going out with Jags.

But can I lose face *and* The Bag of Beauty?

And who said anything about an actual date? Claudia said *go out with*. I could agree to go out with Pinhead, spend five minutes walking down the street on Friday night and win the bet. If FB knows a posh bag's at stake, he'll understand why it appears I've agreed to go out with ASBO boy.

'OK,' I say to a jubilant-looking Pinhead. 'But don't come round. I'll meet you on the corner of Mortimer Road and Talbot Road.'

''Bout seven?' Pinhead leers, and I nod.

And then I hear the buzzer go and look up to see who has come into the shop and why Mr Patel isn't ordering us out.

There's no one on their way in, only FB on his way out, head down, computer mag abandoned on the counter.

Chapter Seven

It's the Friday night at home after the Monday afternoon in the newsagent's, and I am *not* going out with Pinhead for a squillion reasons, mainly because having spent all week discussing the sorry situation with Luce and Sorrel, we all agree that even The Bag of Beauty doesn't merit wasting five minutes of my life on a boozed-up rat-faced hoodie, especially if it means that people think he's the sort of lad I'd choose to go out with. I'd rather be known as a Mega Minger dater than one who dates Grim Reapers, even if it *is* only for a bet.

The other thing that's been worrying me is what's been going on in that little brain of Pinhead's. It's deeply disturbing to think that someone like him is having lustful thoughts about me, which just goes to show you never really know what boys are thinking. In front of you they'll call you names and pretend they hate you, when really, secretly, they fancy the pants off you.

Anyway, I'll be a bit gutted when I see Tits Out sauntering around the place with my bag looped over her pulled-back shoulders, but, quite frankly, I'm not sure that I won't be relieved to get rid of it.

Owning a designer bling bag worth shed-loads of money isn't something I'm finding relaxing. Looking after it takes commitment. When I'm out and about with it I get totally stressed in case I put it down on a piece of gobbed chewing gum, or that someone will nick it, or even that I'm going to be mugged for it and end up with no bag, a seriously bruised arm and, just when the first lot are fading, *more* black eyes. Because it's cream leather there's the risk of it getting dirty, or getting caught in the rain, or someone brushing against it with a cigarette, or the chance that I've left a bit of chocolate in the bottom and it's melted all over the lining.

Quite frankly, the responsibility of owning The Bag of Beauty is more exhausting than owning a pet, and I'm thinking about putting it away until I lead a different sort of life, maybe when I'm Mum's age and don't have to worry about my friends gobbing their gum on it.

I'm also *totally* exhausted and stressed from spending the week avoiding Pinhead, who's after me, and trying to catch up with Freak Boy, who seems to be avoiding me.

I was in the library after school on Wednesday and when I looked up from my essay on Product Extension Strategies I saw FB come in, clock me, and before I could get up and grab him (I was a bit slow, not because I was snoozing, but because my leg had gone to sleep) he'd scuttled out again, which was a shame, not just because I wanted to explain about the whole Pinhead non-date scene, but because even though he doesn't do business studies, he might know something about brand awareness. Now I'll have to ask Mum and hope it's something she's doing on her part-time business studies course at Eastwood Tech.

So, instead of being on a bet-date with a scumbag, I'm lying on my bed, earphones in, iPod on, looking at my bedside clock and thinking of Pinhead standing on the corner, waiting for me, heartbroken that I've stood him up.

And smirking at the thought.

It's just as well I'm spending tomorrow afternoon being pampered for Lucy's birthday. I'm so stressed I could do with some serious TLC, not to mention a gloriously golden-brown bod. And Luce got her way so as well as the pamper party at Cloudz, we're off to Giovanni's. The downside is Bella and Tom are coming too, but we're hoping their only role in the evening is to sit at another table and pick up the bill.

I jump as someone pinches my toes.

'Mu-um!'

She's standing at the end of my bed. I hadn't heard her come in, but then I did have *Greatest Rock Anthems* playing at eardrum-bleeding level.

I rip out my earphones.

'What?'

'There's someone downstairs to see you. Some boy.'

I can tell from her face and the curl of her lips as she says *boy* that it's not a geek or a Lurve God, but someone you wouldn't want turning up on your doorstep on a Friday night to see your daughter.

I stomp downstairs, and, just as I feared, standing on the front-door mat is Pinhead. His grey hood is pulled over his head and he's carrying a two-litre bottle of White Lightning. With the outside light behind him, he really does look like a teenage Grim Reaper, or more accurately, The Dim Reaper.

'What are you doing here?' I ask, as if I didn't know.

'We have a date, remember?' he growls. 'You was supposed to meet me on the corner at seven.' He leans forward, looks down and gives me a hard stare. Clearly, Pinhead hasn't learnt that girls like to be sweet-talked not threatened into agreeing to a date.

'The fact that I didn't turn up should have told you something,' I point out. 'Like I wasn't coming? Anyway, how did you know where I live?'

'The Beakster told me,' Pinhead says. 'Saw him walking his mutt and *made* him tell me.'

I move closer to Pinhead in what I hope is a menacing way, but as he's so tall it means I'm staring at the word *Nike* across his chest, rather than glaring into his eyes.

'What did you do to him?' I growl, worried that Pinhead had bullied FB into spilling my addy. 'Tell me.'

Pinhead says nothing but just stares past me.

I turn round to see Mum at the end of the banister. She's taking her cardie off, which for normal mums, assuming they're wearing something underneath, wouldn't be a problem. But my mother with the Mighty Mammaries is wearing a white top clearly exhibiting the full extent of her humungous boobs, which are packed into a not very supportive bap-pack.

'Who's this?' Mum asks, looping the cardie over the end of the banister and walking towards us. I'm mortified that she seems to be using her upper arms to tuck her boobs back in, which increases her cleavage crack to gargantuan proportions.

'Stephen Prescott. But you can call me Stevie, or, Pinhead, or whatever you want really.'

As he says this, he doesn't take his eyes off Mum's boobs. His bottom lip is practically brushing the front doormat and for one terrible moment I actually think he might drool.

'Me and Lekky have a date,' he says.

'Don't call me Lekky!' I snap. 'And we did, but we don't.'

'We do,' Pinhead says, clearly *not* heartbroken I didn't turn up, just angry.

'Oh, right,' Mum says. She nods towards the bottle of cider Pinhead is carrying. 'Well, Stephen, about the drink . . .'

'Oh yeah, soz,' he grunts. 'That's dead rude of me.' He unscrews the cap from the cider bottle and hands it to Mum. 'Do you wanna swig?'

This is all going *horribly* wrong.

It's even worse than I thought it could be.

My first date is for a bet with a hoodie-wearing weirdo who's leering at my mum's baps and handing her cheap cider on our doorstep.

I *so* don't want to go out with him, but I *so* don't want him in my house.

'Stay there!' I order.

I take the stairs two at a time back up to my room, snatch my phone, some cash, a jacket and my keys, then I hurtle back down and, despite an earlier resolution not to touch him without gloves, push him out of the door as behind us Mum calls out, 'I want you back by ten!'

'I want to know what you did to Frazer Burns,' I say as we turn in to Talbot Road. 'Tell me or I'll . . . I'll . . . do something terrible to you.'

I was going to say smash your skateboard, but the police kept the one he had on Sunday. I saw them put it in the back of their cop car, and I don't think Pinhead's going to be going to the police station to ask for it back anytime soon.

'Fancy The Beakster, do you?' Pinhead jeers. 'He fancies you. Took me ages to get him to tell me it was number 14. Don't worry, he's still alive, just.'

As soon as this is over, I'm going straight round to FB's to make sure he's OK.

The Dim Reaper and I walk along, saying nothing, him occasionally swigging cider and belching, me keeping well out of his way in case he tries to put his arm round me or something, which, as he has freakily long arms, means I'm practically walking on walls and in hedges to avoid him. Still, I'm on a date with the first lad that asked me out, so without even trying I've won the bet, the bag, and *if* I want it, a date with someone almost exotic. How great is that?

'You fancy some chips?' Pinhead asks as we get near a row of shops. 'I'm starving.'

I've had lasagne and chips for tea, but at least in public Pinhead isn't likely to jump on me.

'Yes, please,' I say.

'Well, get some for me,' he says. 'And wiv curry sauce. I'm brassic.'

'Get your own chips,' I snap back. I'm not *that* cheap a date.

The queue is long and they're frying a new batch of spuds, but I don't mind waiting inside. It's brightly lit, warm, and away from The Dim Reaper who's outside with his cider and cigarettes. Gibbo and Spud have turned up and there seems to be a lot of laughing and high-fiving as the creeps celebrate something.

Finally, after what seems like an age, the queue shuffles forward.

Someone has their order and is heading towards the door.

And then I see who it is, and he sees me, and I'm not sure what I should do next.

Ignore him?

Glare at him?

Kick him in the shins?

Warren Cumberbatch hovers beside me, clutching a package. He doesn't say anything, just nods, a bit like one of those nodding dogs on the back ledge of a car.

I don't know what to say to this nodding louse who broke my bezzie's heart, so I just mutter, 'Those chips?'

'Nah, a battered sausage,' he says with a shrug before loping out of the shop and into the street.

I'm straight on the phone to Luce.

'You'll never guess,' I say. 'I've just seen Burger Boy.'

'What? Warren? What's he doing at your house?' Luce asks.

'He's not at our house. He was in The Codfather buying a battered sausage.' I move towards the front of the queue. 'I'm there now.'

'What are you doing in the chippy?' Luce asks. 'I thought you were staying in.'

'Well I was, but then Pinhead called round and . . .'

I have to move my moby away from my ear, as Lucy's shriek is so loud.

'Look, I'll explain when I see you,' I say. 'As soon as I've got my chips I'm going home. Happy birthday for tomorrow!'

I take as long as possible to leave the shop with my chips, unwrapped, salt, no vinegar.

When I come out, Pinhead, Gibbo and Spud are sniggering to themselves. Another large bottle of cider seems to have appeared and Gibbo is swigging from it.

'He says your mum has massive bazongas,' Gibbo giggles. 'Do you think yours might get that big? You could model for *Nuts* if they did.'

'Shut up,' I snap.

Spud joins in with the sniggering and snorting, 'And does she have a fella, your mum? I hear housewives are gagging for it.'

There's more smirking and snorting accompanied by some truly disgusting lower-body thrusting from The Dim Reaper.

I'm off. I'm not wasting another nanosecond with these sickos.

I dodge their grubby hands reaching for my chips and start to walk home.

'Hah! You owe me!' I hear one of them jeer behind me.

Pinhead's at my shoulder. He must have run after me. 'Don't go,' he whispers. 'Go on. If you stay, I'll get rid of them.'

For a moment, he seems almost normal for a lanky lad with a tiny head and the IQ of an amoeba. Perhaps all that other yobby stuff is just bravado. And it must be gutting for the girl you fancy to walk off in the middle of what you think is a date in front of your friends. Talk about losing face!

'Give me one good reason why I should,' I say, popping a chip in my mouth. 'You're a jerk, you're freaky and you've disrespected my mother.'

'I'll split the dosh with you.'

'What?' I practically inhale the hot salty chip. 'What dosh?'

'I only asked you out for a bet.' Pinhead reaches down and takes one of my chips. 'I needed some extra cash to replace the skateboard the cops got hold of.'

I knew it! All along this had the mark of a Tits Out Plan C. I'm going to go straight round to her maisonette and beat her about the head with The Bag of Beauty, even if it does wreck it by getting hair styling gunk and fake tan on the leather.

'Yeah, well you can tell Claudia Barnes when I see her she's dead meat!' I yell, pulling my chips away. 'You two must think I'm stupid!'

'What? Miss Jelly Jugs? This had nowt to do wiv her. The lads bet that you was a lezzer and wouldn't go out with me. I won the first bet 'cause you did, but then they bet me double or quits that I couldn't cop a feel of your tits. If you let me, I'll get twenty quid and I'll give you a tenner.'

I'd like to have said something so devastatingly cutting about Pinhead he withers and dies in front of me. I'd like to have told him that I only went out with him because of a bet too. But it's hard to think straight when you just want to run away and cry your eyes out, and your mouth is stuffed full of fried potato.

Pinhead never fancied me. He just fancied making money out of me. Not even the lowest-of-the-low lad fancied me after all. I was just a bet between him and his yobby mates to get me out and get his grubby mitts under my jumper.

'So give us a handful then,' Pinhead says, lunging towards me, hands outstretched, his skeletal fingers waggling.

I may have wanted to run away and cry a nanosecond ago, but now I'm like a wounded animal, hurt and ready to lash out.

'You numbnuts!' I scream, pushing him away, disgusted. I start pelting him with chips, although, if I hadn't had chips for tea I might have thought twice about using them as vegetable missiles. 'Get away from me, you freak!'

'Hey! Leave off him!'

Gibbo's arrived, elbowing his way in, trying to grab the chips off me.

I try to snatch the chips back – after all, I've paid for

them – but only manage to grab the bottle of cider and in the confusion hurl it towards Pinhead.

Except Pinhead has moved, and in his place is a community policeman, soaked in White Lightning.

When Mum hears my key in the lock she shouts up the stairs from the kitchen, 'Electra, is that you? You're home early!'

'You'd better come up,' I croak, showing the stern-faced policewoman into the front room, which, as usual, looks as if a bomb's hit it.

I throw some magazines and ironing off the sofa, but the policewoman stays standing, her radio crackling.

Mum and Phil come in.

'What's happened?' Mum cries. I'm grateful she's put her cardie back on so her boobs are undercover. 'Has there been an accident?'

'And you are?' The policewoman takes out her notebook.

'Ellie Brown. I'm Electra's mother.'

'And you're the father?' She looks at Phil, who shakes his head. He's still in his AA uniform, so he must have just come back from a shift. He's always doing overtime at the moment *and* he's sold his motorbike. I can't think what he spends his money on, but he must be hard up.

'Well, Mrs Brown, your daughter was involved in a fracas outside the local fish and chip shop.' The policewoman consults her notebook. 'The PCSO reported that, as well as chips being thrown and screaming, there was underage smoking and drinking. He was hit in the thigh by a bottle of cider thrown by your daughter. You are aware that this force takes a zero-tolerance approach to antisocial behaviour?'

Mum's face is a picture, though unfortunately not a very pretty one. I daren't even look at Phil. I expect he's so angry his designer stubble is smouldering.

'Electra?' Mum's voice sounds serious. 'What have you got to say?'

'It wasn't like that,' I say, sobbing. 'I didn't drink, honestly, and I only threw the chips because . . .' I look around the room. It's no time to be coy or spare anyone's feelings. 'They were going on about the size of your boobs.' I nod towards Mum, but I don't look at her. 'They were dead rude, Mum.'

'Well, I should be flattered that you're defending me,' she says, 'but I get the impression we're not getting the whole story.'

She knows me too well.

'I found out Pinhead – that's Stephen Prescott – bet the others that he could feel my boobs.' I up the sobbing level. 'Pinhead tried to grab them, Gibbo – Paul Gibson – he tried to grab the chips and I tried to grab them back but got hold of the cider bottle by mistake and it went all over that policeman.'

'And what about the other lad?' the policewoman asks, flicking through her notes. 'Simon Green. What's his involvement?'

I think of little round Spud with his seriously flaky skin and feel a bit sorry for him. I'm sure he's only turned into a yob because his only friends are Pinhead and Gibbo.

'He's not as bad as the others.'

'But what were you doing out with those sort of lads anyway?' Mum asks, handing me a tissue, which has been stored in her sweaty cleavage so is already a bit damp. 'They're not the sort you usually go around with, are they?'

I shake my head.

'And weren't they the lads involved when the skateboard went into the road last Sunday?'

I nod.

'All three of them are already known to us, Mrs Brown,' the policewoman says. 'Stephen Prescott is very close to getting himself an antisocial behaviour order.'

'Electra?' Mum prompts. 'What's behind all this?'

Three sets of serious adult eyes stare at me.

I'm cornered.

'I only went out with him because Claudia Barnes bet me I wouldn't,' I blurt out. 'She bet me my designer bag I wouldn't go out with Pinhead.'

I can hear all three grown-ups take a sharp intake of breath, as if they're about to choke on a boiled sweet.

'It seems to me a lot of silly betting has been going on,' the policewoman says, snapping her notebook shut. 'Electra, I've been to road accidents where people have been killed because of bets over how fast the driver could go, or a river where a kid has drowned after a bet that he couldn't jump from a bridge. Count yourself lucky that your bet only ended in tears and cold chips.'

'Is that it?' I say. 'You're not going to arrest me?'

For the first time the policewoman smiles. 'I don't think being a bit silly is an arrestable offence, but promise me you'll stay clear of the likes of Messrs Prescott, Gibson and Green, and that you won't make any more daft bets.'

'I promise,' I say, sniffing back snot. I'm not going anywhere near *any* of them, and I'm off making plans or agreeing to bets for *life*.

'I'll see you out,' Phil says as the two of them leave the room.

I sit on the edge of the sofa and feel mega-miserable. First dates weren't supposed to start with an ASBO-kid and end with a police escort home.

Mum's first to break the silence.

'I don't think what happened was entirely your fault, Electra, but, even so, I want you staying in tomorrow.'

'You're grounding me!' I shriek. 'That is *so* unfair! I didn't do anything! And I can't miss Lucy's birthday party. Bella's arranged everything!'

'You *did* do something wrong.' Mum snaps. 'You agreed to a ridiculous bet, and that's twice in a week you've been involved with the police.'

'Oh please, Mum! I won't be on my own tomorrow!' I plead. 'I won't be without an adult at any time. Do you honestly think Bella's going to let me go mental with the breadsticks?'

Mum thinks for a moment. I can tell she's thinking because her forehead is wrinkling and her eyebrows are twitching. Then the wrinkling and twitching stops and I'm pretty sure she's going to let me go when,

'You used Bella as a false alibi once before.'

Phil has waited until now to pipe up with this *so* unhelpful info.

'Don't you remember, Ellie? Electra made out Bella was going to be around the night we went away and the house got trashed.'

Oh well done, Phil. Not only are you trying to

persuade my mother to ground me when she was about to let me off, but you've dragged up the whole party incident again when we could all have totally forgotten it, if it wasn't for the cigarette burns still on the kitchen table and Google's grave in the garden.

'You're right,' Mum says. 'I'll go and ring Bella to check.'

As Mum goes downstairs to use the house phone I get up to go, but Phil touches my arm as I'm at the door.

'Electra, your mum doesn't need any hassle at the moment. I don't want her upset.' There's a warning tone to his voice, but then perhaps he's feeling powerful, still being in uniform.

'Why? Is Grandma ill again?'

Grandma Stafford, Mum's mum, is getting over bowel cancer but, from what Mum said, after the chemo and the op she was going to make a full recovery.

'Of course not,' Phil says. 'But just take it easy, OK?'

Chapter Eight

I'm in Bella Malone's Beast Car, a huge silver 4x4 that would have Yolanda slapping her *Gas Guzzler* stickers all over it, when my phone bleeps.

'It's from Tits Out,' I announce, reading the text. 'She wants to know whether I went out with Pinhead last night.'

'What did you call her, Electra?' Bella asks from the front of the car. I expect her eyebrows would like to shoot up into her forehead, but Luce says her mum's been having a bit of Botox, so they're probably frozen to the spot.

I ignore Bella and stab *Y* on the moby keypad and press *Send*.

Almost immediately, Claudia's blazer-covered boobs are flashing on my screen.

'How do I know you went out with Pinhead?' she

demands. 'I've got no proof.'

'I could get the policewoman who arrested me to give you her report,' I say sarkily, secretly rather thrilled that it all sounds so dramatic. 'She'd confirm I was outside the chippy with Pinhead.'

'You were arrested?' Claudia gasps, sounding dead impressed. 'What for?'

'He tried to assault me.' I wish I'd thought of saying this last night when the copper was in our front room as, whatever way you look at it, uninvited attention in the chest area is assault, even though I'm not *totally* sure whether Pinhead got a feel of my boobs, my chips or a combination of both.

'No way!' Claudia shrieks. 'But if he assaulted you, why were you the one who was arrested?'

'I chucked chips and cider at him, but hit one of the police support guys instead,' I say. 'And they didn't actually arrest me, but a copper came home with me and gave me a caution.' It's not an official caution but as good as.

'That is *so* cool!' Claudia coos. 'Is Pinhead in custody for attacking you?'

'I don't know where he is,' I say. 'Probably back under a damp stone.'

'So you keep the bag and get the date with Jags,' Claudia says. 'Well done, fair's fair.'

As I didn't intend to go out with Pinhead I'd put the thought of a possible date with Jags out of my mind, but if Claudia's going to arrange it, well, it would be daft to look a gift horse, or rather a Spanish stallion, in the mouth.

'Yeah, a bet's a bet, Claudia,' I giggle, snapping my phone off. I may have promised the policewoman I wouldn't make any more bets, but it doesn't mean I'm not going to collect my prize, even if it is a bet date with a greasy munchkin.

'I didn't like the sound of that conversation,' Bella says tartly. 'Tits Out. Arrests. Cider. Assault. Betting. It all sounds *very* unsavoury. No wonder your mother's worried about you.'

'She didn't start it,' Sorrel says, sticking up for me. 'None of that was Electra's fault.'

'It never is,' Bella says primly. 'I thought you'd got over all that.'

'Over all what?' I ask.

'Attracting trouble. Getting into scrapes. Your appalling fourteenth party last July was one of the reasons Tom and I decided not to let Lucy have her fifteenth at home.'

'But I didn't want a party at home,' Lucy protests. 'I just wanted to go out with the girls. On our own,' she adds pointedly.

'Lucy, I have worked hard to make this birthday a special one,' Bella says in her clipped Control Freak tones. 'Things have been arranged.'

'What things?' Luce asks, but Bella doesn't answer. Knowing the Control Freak, she'll have organized today right down to the moment we sit around a cake with colour-coordinated icing and candles to sing 'Happy Birthday'. I'm surprised she hasn't had us round to the house for a pitch-perfect rehearsal.

We zoom along in uneasy silence until Luce swivels round and says to me, 'Did you tell Sorrel you'd seen Warren?'

Oh right, Luce, just invite Sorrel to vom all over your mother's grey leather seats, why don't you? Is vomit-covered upholstery your revenge for Bella taking over your birthday celebrations?

'You never said,' Sorrel says to me, showing no sign of even the smallest retch. 'Where?'

'Last night, in The Codfather.'

She runs her teeth around her right thumbnail. 'Did he say anything?'

'A battered sausage.'

'What? Just a battered sausage?'

I thought Sorrel might be so mad she'd want to stop the car, hunt Warren down and batter *his* sausage, but she sounds mega-relaxed.

'Yeah, he was on his way out and I asked him if he had chips and he said, "Nah, a battered sausage."'

'And was he with anyone?' Sorrel asks. 'What size portion did he have?'

'From the size of his package he only had one battered sausage,' I say. 'He defo wasn't with Jas, if that's what you're wondering.'

As a vegan, Jas wouldn't be seen dead with a meaty sausage of any description.

'Interesting,' Sorrel says, and then slides down in her seat and starts fiddling with her moby.

'Did you get a birthday card from Pascal?' I ask Luce, trying to change the subject. 'Was it French kisses on a card?'

'The Frog forgot,' Luce says flatly.

'You don't know that, Lucy.' Bella is trying to park The Beast Car outside Cloudz between two cars. The gap's so small the parking sensors are going mental. 'There's probably a perfectly good reason why there's no card.'

'I don't care,' Luce says. 'I've gone right off him anyway. Pascal is so last summer!'

We lurch backwards and hear a crunching sound and the noise of shattering glass. Bella swears, not just a little swear word but a big beginning-with-f one, which is a *totally* un-Bella-like thing to do.

'Just get out and I'll pick you up later,' she shrieks.

'Your mum seemed a bit flustered,' I say as the three of us leave Bella writing a note to the owner of one of the cars, a black thing now with a busted front light and bent bumper. 'I thought the Control Freak was going to totally lose her cool there for a moment.'

'She's been a bit angsty for days,' Lucy says, pushing open the door to Cloudz. 'Like she's had a whole week of PMS.'

'My mum's like that but blames it on the menopause,' Sorrel says. 'She says her periods are all over the place and her oestrogen levels are plummeting.'

I have absolutely no idea of my mother's periods *or* her oestrogen profile, and I'd like to keep it that way, thank you very much.

'Hello, girls!'

A blonde girl with a *seriously* orange face and obviously fake hair extensions greets us.

'I'm Lucy Malone. My mum booked us a pamper party,' Lucy explains.

Extension Girl looks at the appointment book, fiddles around beneath the reception area and then shrieks, 'Ta da!' and, with a flourish, hands Luce a silver plastic crown. 'Happy birthday, Lucy. Welcome to Cloudz, where we turn girls into goddesses.'

If they can turn me into a goddess, it will not only be fantastico, it will be a miracle!

'I'm Charlotte but everyone calls me Shar. Mrs Malone has booked you in for one treatment each, plus Cloudz throws in an extra treatment for the birthday girl and her friends to be selected from this list.'

She pushes a piece of paper in front of us, but we'd decided days ago.

'I'd like a luxury pedicure, please,' Luce says. 'And a manicure.'

'I'd like a full-body fake tan,' I say. 'And a de-stressing head massage.'

'And I want a manicure with stones in the end of my nails,' Sorrel adds. 'And a Diet Coke.'

Shar makes tutting noises. 'Unfortunately, diamanté is an extra with the manicure, and Mrs Malone has specified that we can only add extras with her approval. How about nail art instead?'

After the bad atmos in the car and the parking prang, I don't think anyone wants Shar to ring Bella to ask if Sorrel can have fake diamonds stuck to her nails, so nail art it is.

'Leanne!' Shar calls across the salon. 'Will you do Lucy's

mani and pedi?' She smiles at Sorrel. 'Janelle is just finishing off a Brazilian and then she'll do your nails.' She turns to me. 'And you're with me. This way.'

I look back at the girls and grin as Shar leads me away from the main salon, down a small corridor and into a side room where what looks like a one-sided space pod is standing against the back wall. Any moment now I'll be stripping off and going in a pasty porker only to emerge a glorious golden goddess.

I can't wait! Because of the adult-escort-at-all-times-on-Saturday rule Mum decided to make, I haven't had a chance to go round to FB's and check that Pinhead didn't throw him into a ditch or stick his head in a waste bin to get my address. But tomorrow, when I'm allowed out and about, I'll be straight round with some spurious query about Pythagoras so FB can see my inner goddess is now on the outside. If my legs look like golden thin baguettes rather than thick salamis, I might even change the habit of a lifetime and wear a skirt with no skin-camouflaging thick tights or leggings, even though it's November.

'I just need you to fill out the attached form noting any medical problems or allergies you might have, and any special considerations we should take into account.' Shar thrusts a clipboard towards me. 'I'll be back in a moment.'

I fill in my name and address, and wonder if under the

allergies section I can put aubergines, even if it's not strictly true I'm allergic to them, just that I loathe them, but decide against it, as what's the likelihood of a beauty therapist forcing me to eat vegetables of the devil as part of a fake-tan routine?

Shar reappears. 'Now, what colour do you want to be?'

'What's the choice?' I asking, thinking, *Not yours.*

'There are four intensities: Latte for a hint of colour. Mocha, a medium brown. Espresso a deep nut-brown, and Double Espresso, our darkest level and really only suitable for clients of colour.'

I look down at my pasty arms. 'I'd like Espresso, please,' I say.

'A lovely shade, and my own colour of choice,' Shar coos, and I wonder if it would be rude to say, *Latte! Mocha! Anything but the radioactive Lucozade look!*

'Now, strip off and pop these on. I'll be back in a moment and then we'll start.'

'*We'll* start?' I say, looking at the teeny paper knickers Shar has handed me. '*You'll* be back? Don't I just get in and press a button?'

Shar shakes her orange Day-Glo head. 'This is a therapist-based system where we use a hose to apply the tan. It means we can shade and contour as we go.'

I am *horrified*! However much shading and contouring

of my meaty limbs she plans on doing, there is no *way* on earth I'm going to stand starkers with only a piece of paper between my bits and Shar whilst she blasts me with Espresso.

She must see a look of horror on my face as she trills, 'Don't worry, I'm a professional, I've seen it all before.'

But you haven't seen mine before, I think miserably as I start to strip off. I wish I were outside with Lucy and Sorrel having my nails buffed instead of my body hosed. This is supposed to be a pamper party, not teenage torture.

And it gets worse

They're not paper knickers.

It's a paper thong!

'Oh my goodness!' Luce giggles when she sees me shuffle back into the main salon dressed in a brown towelling dressing gown and plastic flip-flops. 'You look as if you've dived into a jar of Marmite!'

As I'd left the treatment room I'd caught sight of myself in the mirror, and would have wept if I wasn't in danger of making tracks through my Espresso-sprayed face. I look as if I've rolled in mud, my hair is like a bird's nest courtesy of the head massage, which Shar forgot to tell me included lots of oil and vigorous rubbing, and no amount of fake tan can disguise the fact that I've still got a couple of black eyes. Add to that my sturdy limbs and furious face, and I look exactly like a female mud wrestler, which is *so* not the look I thought Cloudz would give me.

Luce is wearing her tiara, sitting in an armchair, sucking a pink smoothie through a straw, her legs resting on Leanne's brown-towelled lap whilst her feet are attacked by a foot file, so whereas I look like a Doctor Who monster, Luce looks every inch the birthday princess.

'It's come up from the deep!' Sorrel says, rolling her eyes as Janelle does things to her cuticles.

Shar points to a wicker chair. 'Sit here and let everything dry for half an hour, take a shower in the morning and by tomorrow you'll be golden brown and your inner goddess will be revealed.'

'I'm a freakin' gargoyle, not a goddess,' I growl at Shar. 'I'm supposed to be going out later.'

Shar looks a bit shocked, though not as shocked as I was when I saw myself.

'Oh dear.' She sucks air in between her teeth. 'If you'd said you had plans I would have advised against your choice of colour. You didn't indicate anything about going out on the form under Special Considerations.'

I contemplate rushing back into the treatment room,

grabbing the form and the clipboard and beating Shar around the head with it.

'It doesn't matter,' Luce says. 'It's just me and Sorrel and Mum and Dad at the restaurant. We don't mind how you look.'

Bella minded how I looked.

When she came to pick us up and pay the bill she refused to let me sit in her car without protection. I'd had enough of Cloudz so I stood in the street, in the cold, doing a great impression of a tramp, whilst Bella went to a local shop and bought a roll of black plastic bin liners. I've got my clothes on, but she's clearly worried in case I start rolling around on the back seat and rub my muddy face and hands on her precious leather.

'I can't go out like this,' I wail to Luce as we pull into the drive of her house, a large modern pile on a private road. 'I'm traumatized. I've post-tanning traumatic stress syndrome.'

'Electra, you are the only person I know who can have a fake tan at someone else's expense and come out traumatized,' Bella says, turning off the ignition.

I'm not sure whether she's trying to be funny or not, but whatever she says, I *am* traumatized because I keep remembering the paper thong, lack of a bra and getting goose pimples *all over* when the cold spray hit me. My boobs are small enough without them shrinking from the cold.

'Can I have a shower, Bella, *please?*' I say, getting out of the car and retrieving my bag from the boot. It's got Lucy's birthday present and a change of clothes as I had intended to go to Giovanni's looking like a teenage temptress just in case the waiters were exotic and lush, but, courtesy of Shar and her nozzle, I'm a teenage tramp.

'You know you'll wash it all off?' Sorrel says, admiring her nails, which even in my state of post-traumatic-self-tan stress I can see are totally gorge. Blood red with tiny silver stars all over them.

'I don't care,' I whinge, thinking that at least it's not *my* money going down the drain, literally, and how humiliated I'd feel if the staff at Giovanni's made me sit on a plastic mat.

'I'm a little concerned about whether the limestone tiles in the shower will stain,' Bella says, letting us into the house. For one terrible minute I think she's going to suggest I stand in the garden whilst she hoses me down, but then she says, 'It'll probably be all right, but you'll have to use old towels.'

Lucy and Sorrel race upstairs to Luce's bedroom.

I'm slightly behind as I'd waited for Bella to dump a

blue beach towel in my arms.

I'm about to follow them, when from the landing above I hear testosterone-drenched voices laughing. It'll be James and some of his mates from King William's. They might only be in the year above us, but in terms of looks and snogability, the boys at KW are generally *way* ahead of the Burke's boys.

'Happy birthday, little sis of big bro James.'

It's Jags's voice, and years of trying to impress him have obviously left their mark as, like some sort of reflex action, I dart into the coat cupboard to hide my oily grubby bod.

'Have a lovely evening!' one of the other boys calls out as they come down the stairs, sounding like a herd of stampeding elephants above me.

'Mu-um!' James shouts. He's on the other side of the door, in the hall. 'Where are our coats?'

'Where they should be!' Bella shouts back from somewhere within the vast house. 'In the cupboard!'

I know what's coming next and there's nothing I can do about it. I've already pushed myself as far back into the waxed jackets and Puffa coats as I can, and I'm now sitting on a set of golf clubs, practically skewering my bum with what could be a five iron.

And, sure enough, the door opens, a hand fishes

through the pile of coats, takes a bundle and reveals me, fully dressed but feeling more naked than I did when I was only wearing my paper thong.

'Lucy!' James calls out, staring at me. 'It's your crazy friend.'

The other lads peer at me and collapse with laughter.

'Hey, dude!' Jags laughs. 'You've got a swamp monster living under your stairs!'

During all the time I've fancied Jags, he's rarely noticed to me. For years he never spoke to me, calling me *The friend of James's kid sister* and once *Dude*, which was mortifying as he only calls boys dudes, which means he didn't even realize I'm female. Mostly he completely blanks me, though last summer he remembered that I was the girl who pulled his jeans down, not in lust, but to try and break my fall when I accidentally got so drunk I could no longer stand up.

But with Swamp Monster we've hit an all time low.

Even if Claudia pushes her boobs out, flutters her eyelashes and promises Jags anything she can think of and he might want, he's not going to date a Swamp Monster.

But do you know what? I don't care! I don't want to spend my precious life lusting over a boy who doesn't spend even a nanosecond lusting after me, even when I'm not in Swamp Monster mode. I can't think what I ever saw in him. I'd rather go out with FB and I *never* thought I'd say that!

Bella appears, followed by Luce and Sorrel.

'I suppose I shouldn't be surprised you're hiding in our cloakroom, Electra, but even for you this seems a strange thing to do.' Bella's voice is tight and clipped. 'Is there anything you want to say?'

I look at Bella who's standing with her lips pursed, arms folded across her chest, the expensive highlights in her blonde bob quivering with indignation. Luce and Sorrel are trying their best not to giggle as, behind them, Jags, James and two lads are chasing each other round the hall with their coats over their heads, pretending to be a swamp monster, in other words, me.

'I'm off for a shower,' I say, walking out of the cupboard, my Espresso-and-oil-drenched head held high.

Chapter Nine

Lucy is over the moon with the jewellery box shaped like a pair of red lips I gave her, and the set of five different-coloured enamel bracelets Sorrel put in it.

Sorrel is thrilled with her blood-red silver-starred nails and has obviously cheered up, as she announced on the way to Giovanni's that she's got her appetite for flesh back and wants a juicy steak, cooked rare, with masses of chips to mop up the blood.

I am not thrilled about *anything*.

I've washed my fake tan off but not the oil from my hair, and my head feels even more stressed than before I had the de-stressing head massage.

Tom Malone can't find anywhere to park near Giovanni's and starts swearing about people driving huge cars that take up loads of space, a bit rich given that Bella drives a huge Beast Car and Tom's Mercedes estate isn't what you might call *compact*.

'Oh for goodness' sake, Tom,' Bella snaps, sounding majorly stressed. 'Just drop us at the door and go round again. We're late already.'

Despite the paper-pants events of the afternoon, I have to say that I feel excited about walking into Giovanni's. The nearest the Brown family ever get to Italian food is a pizza in Pizza Hut or a Marks & Spencer deep-filled lasagne. Giovanni's is a *real* Italian, not one where you're likely to take home your meal in a box or be offered a side order of garlic mushrooms if you buy a deep pan and a large soft drink.

A man with a dark suit and wavy black hair greets us at the door.

'Ah! Signora Malone and the lovely signorina!' He kisses both Bella and Luce twice, once on each cheek. 'Happy birthday! No Signor Malone this evening?'

'My husband is parking the car, Giovanni,' Bella says as Dark Suit takes our coats. 'The traffic is murder out there.'

All the others manage to take their coats off easily, but mine gets wedged over my salami limbs as if I'm wearing a New Look-designed straitjacket.

Seeing me struggle, Giovanni stands behind me and yanks it off, leaving three fake-silver bracelets behind.

'Your waiter tonight will be Umberto,' Giovanni says as

I fiddle around in the coat, finally managing to excavate the bracelets from somewhere around the shoulder seam.

Umberto is hovering, all snaky hips, a little goatee beard and so old, he's practically a wrinkly. So much for lush waiters!

'You follow me,' he orders in such a heavy Italian accent he sounds like one of the Mafia. He leads us through the restaurant, which is dark with flickering candles and red tablecloths. 'Your guests are here.'

Guests? No one said anything about guests. In my gargoyle state, I'm not up to seeing guests!

'SURPRISE!'

Three complete strangers jump up, and for a moment I think we've been shown to the wrong table and the strangers will have to sit down, red faced and embarrassed, and do it all over again for someone else.

But then I see Lucy's face.

Even in the flattering candlelight there's no mistaking her utter horror.

'Bonjour, Lucee. 'Appy birthday.'

One of the threesome is a puny pale-haired boy who looks about twelve. I don't recognize his face, but his blond bog-brush hairstyle is unmistakable.

It's Pascal, Lucy's summer Froggy fling.

He comes over and tries to give Luce a kiss, but instead

of throwing her arms around him and snogging his face off, she looks stiff and awkward, as if she's kissing an elderly aunt with whiskers on her chin. Actually, in the candlelight, I notice Pascal has whiskers on his chin. Just.

'Isn't this fabulous?' Bella gushes. '*Now* can you see why I couldn't have you just going out with the girls? It was all rather last minute, but I knew you'd be thrilled!'

Thrilled? Luce is clearly so horrified her summer foreign fling has turned up here, in winter, she looks as if she wants to run out of Giovanni's and throw herself under the wheels of a passing lorry.

'This is Pascal,' Lucy explains in a tight, thin voice. 'And these are his parents, Bernard and Joséphine.'

Pascal sits down between an enormous woman wearing a purple nylon tent, her mousy hair scraped back into a bun, and a little sultana of a bald man with a battered face, brown skin and deep wrinkles.

'Er, your muvver, she, er, arranged a surprise for your birthday,' Pascal explains in a heavy French accent, nodding towards Bella who is fluttering around hugging foreigners gabbing in what I'm always told (by Bella) is perfect French.

I notice that whilst Bella and Tent Woman are embracing, Pascal takes a big gulp of red wine from his mother's wine glass.

'It certainly *is* a surprise,' Luce says through gritted teeth, firing death rays at her mother as we all sit down. 'I had no idea.'

'And my muvver and favver, er, they thought we should come.' Pascal looks sideways at his parents. He's clearly shifting the blame for this disaster-written-all-over-it visit on to his parentals. 'Eet might be good for, er, business.'

'Business?' Lucy glares at Bella who looks shifty. 'What business?'

'Now the house market's dropped over here, your father's thinking about taking on rental properties in France,' Bella says. 'We thought Joséphine and Bernard could help Home Malone expand into Europe.'

Before Lucy can ram a breadstick up Bella's pert nostril, Pascal pushes a birthday present towards her.

'Thank you.' She smiles a totally false but polite smile and rips off the pink and white striped paper.

It's a book.

A thick book.

'Ooh, lovely,' Luce says. 'Thanks. Just what I've always wanted. The French translation of *Harry Potter and the Order of the Phoenix*.'

I'm practically wetting myself with laughter, and from the look on Sorrel's face she's in danger of feeling damp round her pants too.

Tom arrives and Pascal slugs more vino whilst his parents are being hugged and kissed and backslapped by Tom.

'What do you think of this, young Lucy?' Tom booms. 'Quite a surprise your mother organized for you. Now, let's rearrange everything so Lucy and Pascal can sit next to each other, and we can sit next to Bernard and Joséphine.'

Luce says nothing, and for a moment I think she's going to refuse to move, thereby scuppering the Malones' plans of extending their estate agency business overseas. But then the two sets of parents stand up and start playing musical chairs, so we have no choice but to join in.

Whilst Umberto makes a great fuss of shaking out red napkins and placing them on our laps, Tom is talking in fluent Franglais at a glazed-looking Bernard, Bella is gabbing in French to Joséphine, and Pascal starts making crosses in the butter with a grubby fingernail at which point Lucy glares at us and announces, 'I need the loo.'

Sorrel and I scramble to our feet and head after her.

'What was she thinking?' Lucy squeals the moment we've squeezed into the one loo, me crouching on the toilet lid and Luce and Sorrel standing either side. 'I'll kill her!'

'What were *you* thinking?' Sorrel says. 'He's a right skinny creep. *And* he's knocking back the vino when *Maman et Papa* aren't looking.'

I hadn't actually wanted to say that the boy sitting awkwardly at the table outside looks nothing like the blond, tanned French guy Luce had gushed over when she'd come back from her holiday in Provence. But Sorrel's right. If it weren't for the spiky hairstyle, I'd never have recognized him. He looks like one of the zitty-bum-fluff boys at Burke's, only without the zits, just the bum fluff.

'He looked different tanned and surrounded by lavender,' Luce moans. 'Now he's pale and getting plastered. This is *terrible*. What am I going to do?'

'Be nice to him?' I suggest, which is totally out of character for me.

Perhaps the fake-tan fumes have seeped into my brain.

Despite the shower, Espresso has certainly seeped into my pores.

I had a quick peer in the mirror on the way to the loo and my face looks as if I've got huge blackheads all over it. Perhaps I have, which is something *else* to stress over.

'You don't want him to think you still fancy him,' Sorrel points out. 'Not unless you still do.'

'As if!' Luce splutters. 'He's a weedy wimp!'

117

'Lucy! Are you in there?' It's Bella outside. 'What's going on?'

For a moment I think Luce is going to give Bella the silent treatment so that her mum will have to peer under the door to see whether it's us barricaded in the bogs or someone else with their pants round their ankles – but then she shrieks, 'How could you, Mum? How could you bring that creep over without telling me, just so you and Dad could get your hands on some poxy properties!'

'Lucy.' Bella's voice is low and has a warning tone. 'I suggest you come out immediately.'

'I don't know what I ever saw in him, but I always thought his parents were totally weird.' Lucy pulls a face, puffing her cheeks out. 'Have you seen that purple tent his mum's wearing?'

'You can't miss it,' Sorrel says. 'She's a freakin' giant purple blimp.'

'And his dad's a dead ringer for a sultana!' I add. 'Little, wrinkly and brown!'

'Girls, come out *now*!' Bella sounds as if she means business. I've long since learnt that just because it's your birthday doesn't mean your parents can't have a go at you. No day, not even Christmas Day, is immune from a parental tongue-lashing.

My legs have practically gone to sleep with crouching

on the lid, and the loo handle is sticking into my left butt cheek, so I nod towards the door and we troop out, to find not only Bella standing outside, but the purple blimp too.

Joséphine smiles and nods and manoeuvres her massive frame into the little cubicle as Bella practically frogmarches us away from the door, a strange phrase given that *we're* not the ones from France.

'Thank goodness Joséphine doesn't speak any English!' Bella snaps once we're out of the loo. 'I just hope she doesn't ask me for the translation of giant purple blimp!'

'Mum, I know you meant well, but how could you!' Lucy wails. 'He's a creep!'

'You didn't think that last summer when you were with him, did you? Or what about when you were back and mooching around the house missing him and kissing his photo?' Bella says sharply. 'Now get back in there and start enjoying your birthday party!'

It's a celebratory catastrophe.

I feel gutted for Luce, and actually also for Bella, who clearly thought she was doing the right thing *and* doing business at the same time.

Luce and Pascal have nothing to say to each other and are sitting in silence as Pascal picks bits of white wax off the candle and makes them into little sculptures. So far, there's a sausage dog, a pig and something that could either be a bird with legs or a fish with a long face and fins.

Tom seems to have run out of things to say for once, and, next to him, Bernard's doing a great impression of a bored witless sultana.

Bella is getting more and more squiffy so her French keeps lapsing into English. This, not unreasonably, confuses Joséphine who, wedged in her wooden chair with folds of purple nylon flowing over the arms, now looks like a punctured blimp. She either doesn't notice or no longer cares that her teenage son is constantly grabbing her wine glass and draining it, at which point Umberto rolls his eyes and tops it up.

Even the actual meal was rubbish. I've drunk so much Diet Coke I can't stop burping and I've had better pizzas in Pizza Hut.

Pascal sucked up strands of spaghetti from his spaghetti carbonara, making slurping noises and splattering eggy-cream across his face, globs of which sat quivering on top of the bum fluff on his chin until his mother leant across and wiped his face with her napkin. If Luce wasn't grossed out before, she would be then.

She'd ordered a pizza, the first one on the menu,

a margarita, but hardly touched it, presumably because the sight of her puny foreign snog was making her feel too ill to eat.

I had a calzone but hadn't realized it had pepperoni in it, which always reminds me of sliced pig's penis, which isn't the sort of thing you ever want to eat, posh place or not.

Sorrel devoured most of the garlic bread they brought to start, her meal of steak and sautéed potatoes, and the bits of pepperoni I'd fished out of the calzone and hidden under a napkin on my side plate.

'You've got your appetite back,' I say to Sorrel, who's running a finger around her plate as Umberto clears the table.

'Yeah, I'm back to lovin' the flesh,' Sorrel says with relish.

'So the thought of Warren and meat doesn't make you want to vom?' I ask, suddenly panicking that despite being relaxed about the battered-sausage sighting earlier, the name Warren might still want to make Sorrel chunder. Being sick over the table would just about finish off this disastrous birthday in perfect style, and cause Bella to have a nervous breakdown over the ice-cream bomb studded with fizzing sparklers that Giovanni has brought to our table.

'Nah, quite the opposite,' Sorrel says, giving a coy smile.

Before I can quiz her on what's changed, everyone starts singing 'Happy Birthday' in a combination of English, French and Italian.

It sounds like a pack of howling wolves.

'Isn't this fun?' Bella shrieks as all the other diners clap and raise their glasses to the totally embarrassed birthday girl.

'I'm going to Burger King for my birthday,' Sorrel mutters.

'I could do with some air,' Lucy says, getting up. 'You coming?'

Me and Sorrel get up to join her but, to our absolute horror, Pascal stops making his wax zoo and slurs, 'OK.'

It's absolutely freezing, our coats are inside and even though I'm wearing leggings under my dress, my pins are like columns of ice.

Pascal doesn't say anything and we can't say anything in front of Pascal, so we just stand around for a few minutes, me burping, Lucy still radiating anti-Pascal vibes, everyone shivering. I wish the little Frog would hop off and carry on with his waxworks and furtive drinking. Even in the cold night air, I can smell alcohol on his breath.

'Er, what ees that?' Pascal points to a pub a couple of doors down the road. There's heavy rock music coming from inside, and outside groups of men and women are huddled, smoking.

'A pub,' Sorrel says sarcastically. 'What did you think it was?'

'I'd like to go to a purb,' Pascal says. 'A proper Engleesh purb. With *bière*.'

'You can't,' Lucy snaps, finally abandoning any attempt at being polite or grateful that the Fourniers have made the trip. 'You're fifteen.'

Or so he says, I think to myself.

'So?' Pascal snaps back. 'You are not my muvver.'

He shrugs in a very French and arrogant way, staggers along the pavement and disappears through the doors of The Snooty Fox.

'Now what do we do?' Lucy cries as we follow him, obviously not into the pub, which looks well dodgy. 'What if he comes out blotto?'

'*More* blotto you mean,' Sorrel points out. 'Listen, he's a foreign kid who looks about twelve. I hardly think he's going to be served pints of snakebite with voddy chasers. He'll be chucked out any minute.'

We hang around, just away from the smokers but, despite Sorrel's confident prediction, there's no sign of

Pascal being thrown out on to the street on his bony foreign backside.

'My ears are so cold, they're about to snap off,' I moan. That would be the final straw, going to school on Monday with streaky fake tan, black-ish eyes and no ears. Where would I put my earrings?

'I'll go back and get Dad,' Luce says. 'I'm not spending the last few hours of my birthday hanging around outside a grotty pub. Can you two stay here in case he comes out and staggers into the road?'

Lucy's barely gone when the doors of the pub open and Pascal wobbles out holding an almost full pint glass.

'How you say, cheers!' he declares, lurching towards us and holding up the glass before taking a long and noisy gulp.

'That's someone's drink!' I shriek. 'You've nicked someone's drink.'

''Ave some!' Pascal says, pushing the glass towards me and belching beer and garlic in my face. 'Engleesh girls lurve dreenk.'

'You stink!' I say, wondering if all my encounters with French lads are destined to end in disaster.

I try to push the glass away, but as I do, I feel Pascal let go and instinctively grab it to stop it falling and smashing.

'What's going on?'

It's a woman's voice I vaguely recognize. When I've stopped laser-eyeballing plastered Pascal, I see who's asking the question. It's the policewoman who escorted me home from the chippy last night.

'Rats!' I say under my breath, looking at the policewoman, who's looking at the beer glass in my hand. 'It's not how it looks. Honestly.'

Chapter Ten

It was rather unfortunate the way Bella told Mum and Phil the story when she and Tom ran me home last night.

I don't know whether she was determined to give Mum a heart attack or just couldn't think straight because she was tired, emotional and completely sozzled, but she started off by saying, 'Electra was caught by a policewoman outside The Snooty Fox with a pint of beer.'

It was only when Mum hit the roof, Phil started pacing up and down and I began shrieking, 'It wasn't my fault!' that Bella agreed it wasn't, and told them the full story.

Faced with a British policewoman and his French father, the little foreign creep suddenly lost his ability to speak even the most basic English, so Bella was summoned from the restaurant along with the purple blimp.

There was lots of very fast talking and shrugging and hand-waving between Pascal and his parents but, even in her alcohol-soaked state, Bella was able to translate that what Pascal was telling his parents was that *I* was the one that had gone into the pub, stolen someone's drink whilst they weren't looking and come back out with it. Their perfect son was, according to him, *horrified* at what I'd done. The thieving scroat even made a little speech about how it's well known that British teenagers have a drink problem, though luckily I only found this out in the car afterwards when Bella was telling Tom, or I'd have murdered Pascal but not before demanding he was breathalysed.

Anyway, standing in the street, outside the pub, after Bella told us Puny Pascal's version of events, Lucy and Sorrel exploded and I'd demanded Bella translate: 'Tell the sultana and the blimp that their slimy son couldn't wait to get bladdered!'

I don't know whether Bella did translate it, or whether she couldn't remember the French for bladdered, but after a lot more arguing between Bella, Bernard and Joséphine, and the intervention of a Goth-woman who had been smoking outside and claimed she'd seen the whole thing despite a long black fringe covering her face, Bella convinced the policewoman that I wasn't to blame and she hoped that the law would overlook Pascal's *youthful indiscretion*. Clearly not wanting to spark an international incident between two European countries, the policewoman did, so we all went back to Giovanni's, the French lot grabbed their coats and stomped out of the door, Tom paid the bill, we left, and I suspect the Malones and the Fourniers will never see each other again, which will be mega-relief to everyone, but especially Lucy, who says she feels physically sick that she let Pascal anywhere near her tonsils.

I'd dashed up the stairs to bed the moment Bella, Tom and Luce left to avoid a late-night ear-bashing from Mum, but now it's Sunday morning and although I've stayed in my room as long as possible and it's now practically lunchtime, hunger has forced me downstairs, still in my PJs.

Mum's sitting at the kitchen table surrounded by the Sunday papers.

She glances up as I come downstairs. 'What's wrong with your face? It looks all blotchy.'

'It's a fake-tan fiasco,' I say. 'I'm a gargoyle not a goddess.'

I haven't yet worked out what I'm going to do about school tomorrow, and how I'm going to face going in looking as if I've spent the weekend wallowing in a mud bath. If Mum didn't let me off for something serious like black eyes, I can't see her writing a note to say I need time off because my fake tan's gone streaky. And it's not just because of the tan disaster I'm a blotch-head. I've had a good squeeze of what I thought were blackheads, but were actually pores filled with Espresso-coloured gunk.

I push aside one of the colour magazines and pour myself a bowl of Shreddies. 'Where's Phil?'

'Working,' Mum says. 'Again. And while we're on our own, Electra, we need to talk.'

Uh oh. From the tone of her voice it doesn't sound like the sort of *We need to talk* type talk that is followed by, *about what size patent burgundy ankle boots from Top Shop do you want for Christmas?* more of an *about your behaviour* type talk.

'Before you start, last night wasn't my fault, even though you think it probably was, especially after the stuff on Friday night, and last Sunday. I was just in the wrong place at the wrong time with the wrong people. Again.' I thought I'd get in first to save a slow painful build-up to the parental pasting.

'Well, that wasn't what I was going to say, but now you mention it, you have had three run-ins with the police in a week.' Mum sounds tired rather than angry.

'Er, hello? Like I've been saying, none of which were my fault!' I shriek, splattering the *Mail on Sunday* magazine with soggy Shreddies.

'Calm down, Electra! I'm not saying they've been your

fault,' Mum says. 'I'm just stating the facts. For reasons I don't understand you seem to attract trouble.'

'You sound like Bella Malone,' I grumble. 'She's always saying I'm a trouble magnet.'

'I don't always see eye to eye with Lucy's mum, but at the moment she's right.'

Mum gets up from the table, goes over to the side, flicks on the kettle and leans against the units. She's staring at me as if I'm some sort of streaky pyjama-clad weirdo she's just discovered devouring breakfast cereal in her kitchen.

'I think I should make an appointment with the school,' she says. 'Just to talk things over.'

'If you want to go and see the school, fine, but honestly, Mum, you've got nothing to worry about. I'm trying much harder at school. All the teachers will tell you the same.'

Mum seems surprised that I seem totally OK at the thought of a school visit, but I've got nothing to stress about now. I go to the library not just to snooze but to study, I no longer read *heat* behind my textbooks in class, and whilst I'm still struggling with some of my assignments, now I ask the teachers for help rather than just pretend a dog I don't have has eaten homework I haven't done. So I'm totally relaxed about Mum going to the school – as long as she doesn't talk to my French teacher, The Big Geordie, or Poxy Moxy who takes me for history, oh, and Mrs Frost who teaches us English language and literature because Frosty the Penguin *totally* hates me.

'There's no need for you to see anyone,' I say, deciding that I'm not as relaxed as I was a moment ago, in fact, I'm now consumed with anxiety about what some teachers will say about me. 'What do you think they're going to tell you, anyway? That they have to call the cops when I'm in maths in case I start a riot? That I throw fireworks around in assembly?'

These are actually things that have happened at Flora Burke's, but I've had nothing to do with them.

'I'm not saying *you're* the troublemaker,' Mum snaps. 'I'm just saying I'd like to talk this over with a professional. So, who should I see? Your headmaster, your form tutor, who?'

I shrug. 'Mr Thomson doesn't know me. Miss Kapadia is Head of Girls for Year 10 but she doesn't know me either. Mr McKay knows me but he's got rank breath.'

'So Mr McKay then?'

'Mum! There's nothing wrong!'

She runs her hands through her hair and sighs. 'I'm concerned things are getting out of hand. It's not you, Electra, it's the people around you.'

'Like who?' I say. 'Who do I go round with that's

a bad influence? Luce is Miss Perfect and Sorrel wants to be a policewoman!'

'Well, shall we start with the cider-swigger who was on our doorstep on Friday night, the one who looked as if he'd banged a six-inch nail in with his forehead? Or would you like me to focus on that friend of yours at the doctor's, the one who looked as if she might give birth in the surgery?' Mum sounds really stressy-headed.

'Cassie Taylor?' I say. 'She's not a friend of mine! She's a Year 11 preg-head. I hardly know her!'

'The two of you seemed pretty chummy, and given that it will have taken her nine months to get to the point she's at now, she wasn't much older than you when it happened. I'm your mother. I'm not yet ready to be a grandmother.'

Oh, this is mental!

'I haven't even got a boyfriend, and if I did I wouldn't be stupid enough to get preggers by mistake,' I snap back. 'Only a dimwit gets caught out nowadays!'

'Electra . . .!' Mum's voice has a serious warning tone to it but I plough on.

'And why give me the stressies? Jack's the one who's been the troublemaker. *He's* the one who's stolen things in the past, and yet *I'm* getting it in the neck! I never hear you grilling *him* about becoming a pram-face!'

Hmm. Sometimes my mouth and my brain work at different rates.

'I'm going out!' I say before I can spout any more biologically incorrect rubbish.

It's a shame I didn't get dressed before coming downstairs or I could have just stormed out and slammed the front door. Stomping upstairs to get changed and then stomping out isn't so dramatic, and I'm not so desperate to escape that I'd be prepared to wander around the streets in brushed cotton PJs and no bra in November.

'Electra, we still need to talk,' Mum says. 'I don't want you going out.'

This sounds like an order.

'You're jailing me?' I shriek. 'That is *so* unfair!'

'Don't be ridiculous. I'm not jailing you, I'm just saying there's still things we need to discuss!' Mum is angry now.

I glare at her. I hate it when we have rows, but I'm furious she's not seeing my point of view, and hurt that she doesn't seem to understand *I'm* not the one to blame for all the recent trouble.

'I'm done talking!' I snap. 'You never believe anything I say anyway.'

And then I stomp out of the kitchen and up to my room.

* * *

133

I stayed upstairs for the rest of the day with a chair wedged under the door handle so no one could come in. This isn't so I can snog myself in the mirror in private, it's because I'm *so* not happy. I'm really fed up that I seem to have got into more trouble since I started working harder at school than I did when I was bunking off or leaving homework until the week after it should have been handed in. I've never sworn in front of Mum, never shoplifted. I've only got drunk once and that taught me a lesson, and my pot belly is because of too many Snickers bars and not enough exercise, not because I'm pregnant. And yet, *I'm* getting treated as if I'm a teenage tearaway!

What is mega-annoying is that although I upped the sobbing level to maximum, which you have to do if you have a bedroom on the top floor and a kitchen in the basement and want the parentals to know you're suffering, and even threw a few things around the room – a hairbrush, a shoe, a book on the Second World War – no one even tried to come up to see if I was all right or needed a sandwich, so there was no need for the furniture barricade after all.

So I spent the afternoon in my room, flopping about on the bed, fiddling with the computer, listening to my iPod, half-heartedly doing geography homework, and trying not to think about my rumbling tummy and what FB is up to and whether Pinhead really did bully him on Friday night.

Finally, about four o'clock, hunger forces me downstairs. I need to do some more homework but I can't possibly even think of land masses if I'm famished.

Before leaving my room I settle my face into its *Am I bovvered* look, which is a complete waste of time as when I go down to the next landing I can hear Mum moving about in her bedroom and the sound of Jack playing table football with one of his snotty little friends in his.

So much for grounding me. Mum isn't much of a jailer. I could just walk straight down the stairs and out of the front door, and I would, if I hadn't still got my PJs on, though I have added a grey sweatshirt with an old curry stain down the front.

Downstairs I start rummaging in the fridge.

I've found a cold sausage but I'm having terrible trouble trying to separate slices of wafer-thin ham, when the doorbell goes.

I hear Mum shouting up to my room.

I'm not going to respond. I'm just going to let her go up and find me missing, which will totally freak her out until she realizes I haven't slipped out the door to join an international drug and prostitute ring, but am downstairs raiding the fridge and battling with cured pork.

'She must be down here,' Mum says, as I hear two sets of footsteps come along the hall.

Then I have a terrible thought.

What if it's FB?

What if FB has come round to find out if my eyes are OK or whether I've bumped into any more doors?

Usually when he sees me in a kitchen scenario I'm fully dressed and draped over his parents' cherry-wood units and sparkling granite work surfaces. He's never seen me in my tartan PJs with a cold sausage stuffed in my mouth.

'Hiya!'

It's Tits Out.

She's wearing a white shellsuit with a bright-pink flash across the shoulders, huge gold hoop earrings and giant furry boots that look as if she's strapped a couple of pink yetis to her feet. Her bleached hair is scraped back into a high ponytail revealing ears dripping with earrings, four holes in each lobe.

The last time Claudia was at my house she was sitting on the freezer on the half-landing getting love bites from a lad called Buzzer. I hope she doesn't remind Mum about the disastrous party.

'Last time I was here I was *well* wasted,' Tits Out giggles. She looks up at the light over the kitchen table. 'I remember some of the lads chucking a water-filled condom up there. Sooo mental.'

She laughs at the memory. Oh how I wish I could laugh at it, but I can't and, from the look on Mum's stony face, nor can she.

I contemplate sticking the cold sausage in Claudia's gob before she can come out with anything worse, such as what might have gone on in the other rooms, but as I'm too hungry to waste a good sausage, I gobble it down in three greasy gulps.

'You OK?' Tits Out asks, peering at me. 'Your face looks well grubby. Have you become a weekend soap dodger?'

'I had a fake-tan fiasco,' I say. 'I'm streaky all over.'

'Lemon juice and sugar,' Claudia says knowledgeably. 'But keep it away from your soft bits or you'll be screaming!'

'Do you want to come up to my room?' I've got to get her away from the kitchen and out of Mum's earshot.

'Nah, can't stay, but I was just passing and thought you'd like to know that when I went to buy some chewy from the garage, Bozza Slater said Cassie Taylor had Tequila-Becks on Friday night. Big thing to squeeze out. Ten pounds something. Tore her from front to back. Bet she won't be able to poo for weeks, eh, Mrs B!'

'Tequila-Becks?' Mum queries.

'After the drinks she had when she got preggers,' Tits

Out unhelpfully explains to my po-faced mother. 'Anyway, the real goss is that you know you said she said the father could be Macca Gribben *or* Bozza Slater? Well, some people wonder if it might be Sumo's – you know, the fat lad in Year 11 who's always being excluded – what with it being a huge thing and a bit yellow-looking.'

Claudia screeches with laughter. 'Bozza's dead relieved the chance of it being his might be less, but there'll still need to be a DNA test.'

I can't look at Mum. Her eyes are probably so wide they've burst out of their sockets and are bobbing on her cheekbones.

'Anyway, must go. I met this lad called Pete or Paul or something in the garage, and we're meeting in the precinct later. I'll see myself out.'

And then she and her yeti boots are heading up the stairs, bum wiggling, shouting, 'See you tomorrow!' before slamming the front door.

'And you don't think I'm right to be worried about the people you're hanging around with?' Mum says, her face as hard as the Burnses' granite worktops.

And for once, I agree with her.

Chapter Eleven

We'd been mini-rioting for about ten minutes, just normal stuff, people being pushed off chairs, books being lobbed around, Pinhead mooning out of the window safe in the knowledge that as we're in a top-floor classroom his bare bum is unlikely to be noticed by a teacher, when a man I've never seen before strides into our English class, dumps a pile of papers and magazines on a desk at the front and shouts at the top of his voice, 'QUIET!'

And because he's new and has a loud voice, everyone stops talking. Even Pinhead zips up his trousers and parks his bum on a seat.

'Is, like, Mrs Frost not coming?' Tammy Two-Names asks. As one of the non-rioters, she's already sitting at a desk.

'Mrs Frost is ill,' New Teacher explains.

'I bet her legs have exploded,' Spud pipes up, and

we all fall about with laughter.

Exploding legs as a reason for The Penguin's no-show is a real possibility. Mrs Frost has a terrible water-retention problem and her pins have been getting bigger and bigger over the last few years. We've been speculating for ages just how long her skin can hold all that liquid in place before it splits and showers everyone with bodily fluid. Perhaps it's finally happened.

'What's wrong with Mrs Frost is none of your business,' New Teacher says. 'All you need to know is that I'm Mr Farrell.'

'You a supply, sir?' Gibbo asks. 'Or is you a proper teacher?'

Everyone sniggers.

Lessons with supply teachers are usually dead easy, as they've no idea what you're supposed to be studying. Normally they just give us a book to read and sit at the front of the class whilst we do our own thing, which is never lesson-related and usually noisy and often accompanied by sweets being passed around, and spit-wet paper balls being fired from elastic bands.

'I'm both.' Mr Farrell glares at Gibbo, who actually shrinks back in his seat as if he's being shrivelled by a death ray.

With laser looks like that, I doubt there'll be any

chance of sweet-eating or missile-firing in one of Mr Farrell's classes.

'So, will you be taking us from now on, Mr Farrell?' Claudia's doing her breathy eyelash-batting routine, not because the supply is teacher eye candy, but because she can't help herself when any new man appears, even one with scruffy brown hair, rimless glasses and a stained red tie.

'Maybe,' Mr Farrell says. 'Depends on whether I like you lot or not.'

Everyone laughs and I start to think that Mrs Frost's mysterious illness might not be such a bad thing after all, plus, as Frosty hated me, I've got a whole fresh start with this new teacher.

'OK! Can we have some quiet, please?' Mr Farrell calls out. 'I believe you're about to start a poetry module.'

We all groan and some people even put their head on a desk and pretend to snore. We did a bit of poetry last year and, quite frankly, unless it rhymes, is funny or in a birthday card, like the rest of the class I've never seen the point.

'All right, all right, you've made your views clear,' Mr Farrell says. 'Let's see if we can change your feelings about poetry. I want to show you it can be found in the most unlikely of places.'

I wonder if he's seen the graffiti about our headmaster behind the back of the bus shelter at Eastwood Circle. It's certainly a poem and it rhymes, but I'm not sure it's the sort of verse Mr Farrell had in mind.

'Now, to start, does anyone have any favourite poems they'd like to share with the class?'

No one says anything. If Mr Farrell had taught us before he'd have realized that whilst we can recite dodgy football songs or catchphrases off the telly, poems have passed my Year 10 English language class by.

I swivel round to see who's doing what.

As well as a sea of blank, bored faces, I notice FB sitting near the back, at the side of the room, thankfully a long way from Tammy Two-Names.

I haven't spoken one word to him since the borid incident, and it's not as if I haven't tried. I don't see him for French or maths as we're in different sets, and he doesn't do art or history for GCSE, but even when we have been together in registration, he's definitely avoided me, rushing away when I'm near him as if he's suddenly got a bout of the urgent trots.

'Come on!' Mr Farrell booms. 'Someone must know *something*. Song lyrics? A football chant? Anything?'

'I've got a poem, sir,' Pinhead says. 'It rhymes and everything.'

Mr Farrell probably realizes by the giggles that Pinhead's poem isn't likely to be on the GCSE syllabus, but after he's asked Pinhead his name, he tells him to go ahead.

Pinhead gets up, coughs, flashes a leery smirk and starts.

'There was a young girl from Devizes

Whose boobs were very queer sizes

One was dead small

Almost nothing at all

The other was huge and won prizes!'

Pinhead gives a bow and the class goes wild with laughter, whooping and jeering and banging on the desks.

I'm not laughing.

I'm glaring at Pinhead, who's blowing mock kisses at me.

We both know *why* he's chosen that poem. It's to humiliate me in front of the class. I'm not from Devizes but my boobs *are* odd sizes and Pinhead must have found out when he lunged at me outside The Codfather. He obviously got a handful of boob, not chips.

'OK, that's enough!' Mr Farrell cries above jeers and shouts of *More! More!* 'At least someone in this class could recite something! Right, call me an idealist but I'm sure even you lot have a poetic spirit buried deep within you, and I'm determined to excavate it.'

There's more good-natured jeering.

'As an introduction to poetry we're going to look at love and how it's represented in the media.' He pats the pile of papers beside him. 'For this exercise I want you in groups of about five – so rearrange your desks – BUT before you dive off with your friends, *I'll* do the groups. It will help me learn your names and keep any troublemakers apart!'

Mr Farrell begins to point randomly around the class.

Sorrel's gone to the dentist again, so she's not here.

Luce is with Gibbo, Tam, a pretty girl called Shiluka who I don't think has ever spoken to me because clearly I'm not cool enough, and Dan Metz who I know has never spoken to me as he only has eyes for sporty girls.

Nat is with the original Greek Goddess, Angela Pantelli, flaky Spud and Paul Cottismore, who must be gutted as he's always had a thing for Luce, and from the signs he's making to Sporty Dan is desperately trying to negotiate a swap between tables.

Which leaves me, FB (!), Pinhead, Claudia and Shaz Kamara, who is mad that she's been separated from her bezzie, Shenice Jones, and refuses to help move the desks into clusters or say anything other than, 'S'not fair. S'not fair,' over and over again, whilst pulling pink gum from her mouth in one long spit-covered string.

I go to pick up one end of a desk and find FB's at the other.

'Hi,' I say, realizing I'm grinning like some sort of just-let-out-of-psycho-ward weirdo.

'Hi,' he says shyly, going red above the collar of his white shirt.

'About last week,' I start, but as we move the desks I bang butts with someone behind me, and by the time I've moved the desk, fussed around with my bag and got a chair, my moment with FB has passed and the only space left is between Claudia and Shaz.

'He's a bit lush,' Tits Out says, nudging me as Mr Farrell drops a pile of newspapers and magazines on our desk. 'Take the denim shirt and the glasses off and he'd be quite fit. Not as fit as Buff, but still fit enough for a fumble in the stationery cupboard.'

With or without the shirt I can't see it myself, but I can see that whereas those around us are flicking through copies of *The Times* and *GQ* magazine, we've been lumbered with the *Sun*, a *Radio Times* and lots of out-of-date copies of *Match!*

Mr Farrell tells us to cut out anything we feel represents love, stick them on a piece of card, and make up a statement to go with our collage. The next step is for the class to combine the statements into a poem. At least, that's Mr F's plan.

'Remember, you can feel love for your family, your pets, the environment, a picture, a word. Whatever you feel as a group, reflect it in your statement,' Mr Farrell booms above the noise as he walks around the class. 'As you're going to present your statement and the support for it to the class, give it plenty of thought!'

He passes by our cluster of desks handing out scissors and glue. It's more like art than English, and I'm not sure that giving us sharp instruments is a good idea, not because there's likely to be a fight or a stabbing, but because girls like Claudia and Nat will probably start trimming their nails or snipping their split ends.

'My statement would be: *I'd do her*,' Pinhead sniggers, holding up a copy of the *Sun*, which has a woman in red bikini bottoms with basketball-sized boobs plastered across a page. 'That'll do for me *and* The Beakster.' He leers at FB who's sitting across the table from him. 'What do you think, eh? Shall we tell this supply guy we'd do her?'

'I . . . I don't agree with that statement,' FB says, stammering slightly and squirming in his seat. 'That image doesn't represent love to me.'

'Ooh,' Pinhead jeers. 'You're a right goody-goody, aren't

you, Beakster? But I bet you wouldn't be so goody-goody with Lekky, would you? You do her given half the chance and if she'd let you.'

'Shut up, rat-face,' I snap, jabbing a glue stick towards him in what I hope is a threatening manner and not daring to look at FB. 'You're a pathetic loser! A total jerk!'

'You've changed your tune, Lekky,' Pinhead says. 'On our date you was gagging for me then.'

'Yeah, in your dreams!' I snap. 'Now button it, Pinhead.'

'Yeah, watch it,' Claudia adds, reaching across and grabbing another magazine. 'Electra told me you assaulted her outside the chippy.'

'He did what?' FB says, and this time I *do* look at him.

His hands are shaking and his green eyes are blazing, glaring like lasers across the table at The Dim Reaper. Unlike Mr Farrell's death-eyes on Spud, Pinhead doesn't seem to be shrivelling in the slightest, but starts making obscene gestures with his fingers.

'It was nothing,' I say. 'Just leave it.'

We're supposed to be researching love, but there's a terrible atmosphere of hate brewing around the table, and things feel as if they might get out of hand. I look to see where Mr Farrell is, but he's bending over Butterface's table, showing her how the glue stick works as she's trying to wind up the wrong end.

'Did you belt her? Is that why her face is so red?' Sulky Shaz asks Pinhead, who's still leering over bikini-woman. ''Cause if you did, I'll get my bro and his gang to deck you.'

My face is red because Claudia's lemon juice and sugar tan-remover has not only taken off the fake tan, it's exfoliated the top layer of my skin so that just healing spots have had their scabs blasted off in a sugar and citric acid attack.

'I did nuffink!' Pinhead says quickly, clearly freaked that he might have to deal with Shaz's brother and his thuggy mates in the Eastwood Massive or whatever they're called.

'We all made stupid bets, now just leave it!' I order everyone around the table. I'm desperate to get back to doing things with scissors and glue. 'Let's talk about love and poetry! Let's talk about this Lurve God!' I try to defuse the situation by waving a picture of David Beckham in teeny white underpants in the air.

'He grabbed her boobs,' Claudia says as she casually flicks through the *Radio Times*. 'The police were called and everything, weren't they, Electra?'

'It wasn't like that,' I growl, noticing FB's trembling fingers are now clenched into fists above the desk. 'Just leave it OK?'

'Yeah, I got a right old feel. Bet you wished your sticky mitts had been there, Beakster!' Pinhead leans across the desk towards FB, his hands outstretched and his fingers waggling as if he's pretending to feel boobs in the air. 'Got quite a handful.'

I'm just feeling mega-relieved that Pinhead clearly *didn't* get a feel of my boobs as otherwise he wouldn't have said they're a handful when he adds, 'But not as much as her old ma's. They're like effing torpedoes!'

In a flash FB darts up, leans forward and smacks Pinhead bang on the nose, sending The Dim Reaper flying back on his chair, spindly legs waving in the air. The chair crashes to the ground with Pinhead still in it.

FB scrambles round to the other side of the desk, and for a moment I think he's going to help Pinhead up and apologize, maybe even dust his blazer down, but as Pinhead wobbles to his feet, FB leans over and head-butts him.

Instead of fighting back, The Dim Reaper curls up on the floor, his arms protecting his tiny head, whimpering, 'Get that animal off me! Get him off me!'

'Frazer, don't!' I scream. 'He's a scumbag! He's not worth it!'

FB stands over the moaning thug, looking as if he's going to land another blow. The class abandon their images of love and swarm around, stamping their feet and clapping their hands chanting, 'Fight! Fight! Fight!'

Mr Farrell wades through the crowd.

He grabs FB by his blazer collar just as FB kicks Pinhead straight in his butt-crack.

'Don't you *ever* go near Electra *ever* again!' FB shouts in a surprisingly husky voice as Mr Farrell drags FB away and practically flings him across a nearby desk. 'I mean it!'

'Are you all right?' Mr Farrell helps Pinhead to his feet where he stands swaying, blood trickling from his nose and down his chin. 'You look a bit dazed.'

'He always looks like that, sir,' Shenice says. 'Dazed and confused.'

As the class snigger I glance at FB, who's leaning against a desk, breathing heavily and looking shocked. I really really want to go over to him, but as I make a move, Mr Farrell says, 'And you – Electra, isn't it? What was your role in this sorry tale?'

'Me?' That came out a bit bat-squeaky. 'Nothing!'

'They was fighting over her, sir,' Sulky Shaz drawls. 'Electra had a bet over who could get first cop of her boobs. Pinhead won and Frazer decked him.'

* * *

150

I never ever thought I'd end up sitting on a plastic chair in the corridor outside the headmaster's study, wedged between Pinhead and FB, but that's where Mr Farrell marched us straight after the fight. He's in there now with Mr Thomson, giving his version of events, whilst a random teacher plucked from the staffroom is sitting on the other side of the corridor, watching us in case World War Three starts up again.

Pinhead leans across me towards FB, and for a moment I think round two is underway.

'Nice one, mate. Great right hook. Didn't know you had it in you. Re-spect.' He makes a fist with a blood-smeared hand. FB shrugs and nods back. 'You're defo no fairy. I'll tell Tosser Thomson I wound you up.'

'Thanks,' FB mutters.

'You'll have a right shiner on your nut where you head-butted me,' Pinhead says. 'Mega.'

FB touches his forehead, part of which already has a reddish-purple bruise coming up, and winces. 'Sorry, that was one blow too far.'

'Nah, that was the boot up me arse, but it's OK.'

Unbelievable!

One minute FB is smacking Pinhead in the face, and the next Pinhead is congratulating FB on his nose-busting technique and giving him respect for belting him. Lads!

They're truly from a different planet.

The door to the study opens, and Mr Thomson comes out.

'Hardly the three wise monkeys, are you?' he says sarcastically, doing his teapot impression, one hand on his hip, the other pointing at us as he looks us up and down. 'As you're usually at the centre of things, Prescott, we'll start with you.'

Pinhead gets up and follows Mr Thomson in, but at the door he turns, grins and gives the respect fist to FB again.

'This is terrible!' I moan when the door closes. 'I'm going to have to sit in front of Tosser Thomson and that new teacher and discuss the fact you were fighting over my family's boobs. How embarrassing is that? And what am I going to tell my mum? She's already worried I get into trouble too often!'

'Sorry,' FB mutters. 'I'm not proud of myself. Violence is never the answer but your boyfriend's been winding me up for months.'

'He's not and never has been my boyfriend,' I snap so loudly, the random teacher looks up from his marking. I lower my voice. 'I don't know why you think that.'

'Because he asked you out when we were in the newsagent's? Because you said yes? Because you went out with him on Friday night? Sounds like a boyfriend to me.'

'Oh for God's sake, it was *you* I wanted to go out with in the newsagent's,' I hiss. 'I was hoping *you* were going to ask me out when Claudia and Pinhead came in.'

There's silence and then, '*You* wanted to go out with *me*?' FB gasps, sounding gobsmacked. Then he smiles, and with his hair all ruffled, his tie half undone and his blazer practically off his shoulder, he looks as hot as he did soaked in water the day I saw him bathing Archie. 'If I'd have asked you out, you'd have said *yes*?'

'Yes.' I roll my eyes and grit my teeth, as I can hardly believe I'm saying it. 'I thought something might have happened after the Archie incident, but you avoided me.' I realize I'm making it sound as if this is all FB's fault, but I'm fed up and freaked out.

'I thought *you* were avoiding *me*,' FB says. 'But anyway, if you wanted to go out with me, why did you agree to a date with that thug? Why not just say *no*?'

'Because he asked me out first,' I say.

'So?' FB says. 'You could have still said no.'

I let out a deep sigh. 'Claudia Barnes bet me my designer bag that I wouldn't go out with the first boy that asked me. I thought she might set me up with a Mega Minger, so I thought if I could get you to ask me out first that would solve the minger problem. I'd win the bet and keep the bag. You were my Plan B.'

One look at FB's face tells me I've said the wrong thing.

A moment ago, he was smily and *totally* hot.

Now his eyes, his mouth, every inch of his face shows he's hurting. Badly.

'Frazer, that didn't come out right . . .' I touch his arm, but he pulls away. 'I should have explained it better, told you about the mirror, seeing you all wet that time with Archie . . .'

Frazer cuts me off. 'You wanted to go out with me to win a bet?' His voice is barely a whisper, his head bent over his lap as he wrings his hands. 'You wanted to go out with me to win some stupid bag?'

'It wasn't a stupid bag, it was a Chloé,' I say a little too indignantly. 'But it wasn't like that! I mean, I wanted to go out with you anyway. I wanted to go out with you even when I didn't admit it to the girls 'cause they thought you were off the freakometer. I've thought you were fit for ages, way before Tammy started fancying you.' I'm gabbling. My brain is scrambled. I know I'm digging my own grave with each word I utter. 'Honestly, it sounds worse than it is!'

FB turns to me and looks at me with his gorgeous hurt green eyes. I *so* want to put my arms around him, snog his face off, tell him that I've stopped dreaming of running through cornfields with Jags, and now dream of frolicking in the sea with him and not just because he'd be drenched in water. But I'm not sure that snogging outside the headmaster's office when you're already seriously in trouble would go down well, so I sit on my hands and bite my lip.

'Tell me one thing truthfully, Electra,' FB says, as from behind the headmaster's door I can hear Mr Thomson's raised voice as he gives Pinhead a verbal pasting. 'The day you bought the gardening mag, the one in the newsagent's where we laughed about the word borid, you were trying to get me to ask you out so that you could win the bet with Claudia, weren't you?'

I say nothing. There's nothing I can say. He's already guessed the truth.

I start to weep.

'In other words, you were using me.' Frazer's voice is no longer a whisper but deep and harsh and hurt. 'I thought you were different, but it turns out you're just as stupid and shallow as all the others.'

Chapter Twelve

'That's it. Other than to go to school I don't want you going out from now until Christmas,' Mum snaps, furiously ripping a parking ticket off the car's windscreen.

As it turned out, there was no need for me to worry about how I was going to tell Mum what had happened. The school did it for me. They rang her and asked her to come in immediately, which is presumably why she abandoned the silver Ford Focus in a residents' parking bay when we reside about five miles away.

'But it's only the 19th of November!' I cry. 'I can't stay in for over a month! I'll miss out on all the Christmas stuff! It's not fair!'

'And it's not fair that you seem to keep getting into trouble when it's not your fault, Electra, but that's the way it is,' Mum says, getting into the driver's side. 'Life's not fair. Start dealing with it.'

156

She slams the door and I climb in the passenger side and give Mum a sidelong glance, trying to assess from the state of her chin whether I should carry on with my whinging and pleading or give up. A hard-set jutting chin means there's no hope of any change of mother-heart, whereas a slightly softer chin-pulled-back-into-the-neck look is perhaps worth another go.

As we drive away, I can see that Mum's chin is jutting out so far it could actually toot the horn, so I slump down in my seat and say nothing.

As we drive along in stony silence, I think back to the events of the last few hours.

Pinhead has been excluded from school for two days, which doesn't seem much of a punishment to me as it means that no one at Burke's has to put up with him, and he gets two days lying around at home watching daytime telly, picking fluff from his belly button or something equally disgusting.

FB's been excluded for five days, because although Pinhead wound FB up, FB attacked Pinhead first and carried on slugging him when The Dim Reaper was lying bleeding on the floor, and that, apparently, merits an automatic exclusion. Unlike Pinhead, I expect FB will be gutted about the exclusion, as it will be on his school record.

Everyone agreed that whilst the bag bet started everything off, the actual fight was nothing to do with me, so whilst Miss Kapadia stood and cleaned out her thumbnails with a fingernail, I just got a lecture from Mr Thomson about protecting my assets, by which I think he meant not to make stupid bets about who could touch my boobs or get my bag. I was still sobbing over hurting FB and so freaked that I'd ended up in the headmaster's office I didn't have the energy to tell him that he'd got *totally* the wrong idea, and that however stupid I've been in the past I would never *ever* make such a bet, even for all the designer handbags in the world. So I just stood there snivelling, wishing I'd put waterproof mascara on this morning, my face already sore from the lemon and sugar combo, stinging from my salty tears.

I pull the sun visor down and slide the mirror cover across. My face looks like a slapped backside with a couple of spiders crawling down it.

As Mum and I were waiting to see Mr Thomson, FB's father, Duncan, came out of the headmaster's study. He looked hunky and gorgeous but *very* annoyed. He saw me outside the door, and although I tried to say hello, well, more of a snotty half-smile-and-shrug, he just glared at me and walked away, FB scuttling after him, head down, shoulders hunched, saying nothing, not even giving me a backward glance.

I've *got* to contact FB and explain to him that I didn't mean what I'd said, and that because I was feeling so freaked and stressy, it came out all wrong. I can't bear the thought of him being upset over something that isn't true, well, not in the way he thinks it is. But if I can't go out after school, and he's excluded from it until next week, how am I going to do it?

'Can you just drop me off outside a house in Compton Avenue?' I say, spitting on a tissue and wiping away the mascara spiders. 'I'll just run up the drive and be five minutes.'

Mum takes her eyes off the road to glare at me as we whizz past the entrance to FB's road.

I'll take that as a *no* then.

As I'm under house arrest and don't have FB's moby number or his email address, I'm going to have to resort to dinosaur technology to contact him.

The landline.

Back in my bedroom, I fire up my laptop, find Directory Enquiries, type in Duncan Burns, 7 Compton Avenue and the phone number pops up.

As I stab the numbers into my moby and the phone

rings, I panic and cut the call.

What am I going to say? *Frazer, when you were sitting in the corridor about to be given the third degree by Tosser Thomson I thought you were the hottest thing I've even seen, other than David Beckham, and I wanted to snog your face off?*

Even just a simple *sorry* doesn't sound right, but I've got to do it. However stupid I sound or whatever my potty mouth comes out with, I *have* to speak to FB and try, somehow, to make amends for the dreadful mess I've got him into. Even if he never wants to speak to me again, I have to let him know that I never meant to hurt him.

I press redial.

'Fiona Burns.'

It's the clipped tones of FB's mum.

'Um. Hello. Er, is Frazer in, please?' My heart is thumping so wildly in my chest, I wonder whether FB's mum can hear it and can tell I'm about to have a heart attack. She is a doctor after all.

'Who is it calling?'

'Electra. Electra Brown.' My heart is about to explode and my throat is bone dry.

'Ah, Electra.' Doc Burns's voice is tight and icy. 'I think perhaps it's best if you don't contact my son for the foreseeable future.'

'But!'

'I can't stop you seeing him at school, of course, but out of academic hours, well, let's just leave it for now, shall we?'

I realize that along with my mum and Bella Malone, Fiona Burns thinks I'm a troublemaker.

'Dr Burns, I'm not as stupid and shallow as you and Frazer think I am. It's like when you saw that girl outside your house the other Sunday, it wasn't a pregnant tart, it was me!'

Oh no! What am I saying?

I'll try again.

'Even my mum agrees it's not my fault I keep getting into trouble. And at least this time the police weren't involved.'

I should have written a letter. At least that way I could edit my mistakes.

'Will you at least tell him I called to say I'm sorry?'

Doc Burns doesn't say anything for a bit and I don't want to let my potty mouth say anything else, so there's just a crackle on the line before she eventually says, 'Electra, please don't contact us again. I'm sorry, but both Frazer's father and I agree it's for the best.'

There's a click, and a buzz, and she's gone.

I sit on my bed and stare at the pink walls in disbelief.

My mum thinks my friends are a bad influence on me

and FB's mum thinks I'm a bad influence on him! Is this what happens when you're a teenager? Your parents think everyone around you is out to corrupt their little darling, leading them into a life of swigging cheap cider, getting pregnant and starting fights in classrooms?

I've got the Internet running on the laptop so I open my emails. There's one from Maddy. She must have sent it last night.

To: SOnotagreekgirl1
From: Madaboutnewyork
Date: 18th November 19:42
Subject: *Miracle Mammaries Will Soon Be Yours!*

Hi!

I have sitting in a bag next to me the greatest invention since the last greatest invention (the Internet? cell phones?) – the bra I promised you. Sorry not to get it earlier. Max and me went to a Victoria's Secret on Saturday and got it (and loads of other stuff for us!) so I'll stick it in the mail on Mon and as soon as you get it, stick it on your bod, look down and prepare to be amazed.

What's brewing at your end?

Luv Maddy xxx

Thanks! Can't wait to get the boosting bap-pack. Seriously need something to cheer me up. Involved, sort of, in fight at school between FB and Pinhead (the guy with the spray can that you saw). Have totally nuked any chance of FB romance. He now hates me and I hate myself for telling him I only wanted to go out with him to win the bag bet I told you about. Didn't mean it to come out like that, but it did, and now I'm sunk. Am grounded, banned from seeing him and have been banned from contacting him by his snotty parentals. Am under house arrest from now until Christmas. As I am officially a social hermit bra will have to be worn to school and in the house, not parties. Soz if I sound so D-pressed.

Love Electra xx

Chapter Thirteen

'One Brian's Big One, please,' Claudia says, sticking her fingers through the chain-link fence that frames our playground. She pushes some money to Flyin' Brian who's outside in the street, doing his Tuesday burger run.

'Comin' up, gorgeous!' Brian grins as Claudia wiggles her chest and flutters her eyelashes, probably not so that Bri will ask her out, but in the hope that he might give her extra fried onions and, possibly, a double squirt of tomato sauce on her burger.

This corner of the playground is packed with kids who've had enough of school canteen tuna and salad lunches, and would sell their grandmother to get a greasy burger in a bun. Flyin' Brian used to go to our school before he was expelled, but now it's rumoured he earns more than a teacher by flogging junk food through the fence. He started with a bike and a basket, but things are obviously going well as he's now got an old van, a driving licence and a whole menu of saturated fat and carbs to choose from.

Flyin' B slaps a wrapped burger against the fence and Claudia pulls it through. The burger is bigger than the gap, so there's quite a bit of squishing of bun and folding of meat in order to get it through to the other side.

'Same for me, please,' I say, sticking my chest out, which today is a particularly magnificent chest as the Yankee air bra Maddy sent me arrived yesterday.

It's fantastico.

At first I was a bit disappointed that she'd sent me a flesh-coloured one as it's not very pretty, and, lying on my bed when I opened the package, it looked a bit medical, the type of bra you'd buy if you didn't have any boobs at all or were the sort of weirdy bloke who wished he'd been born a girl. But strapped on, it's like having a couple of balloons in front of me, and the flesh colour means I can wear it under my white school shirt. Several girls asked me where I'd bought it when I unbuttoned my shirt in the loos to show them, so I'm seriously thinking of doing what Flyin' Brian does but with underwear: importing American air bras and selling them through the railings at schools. I might have to fling them over the fence, as I can't see a 34D padded bra fitting through the chain link, however much I squash it.

Even with the miracle bra, Brian doesn't notice my boobs or call me gorgeous, but just sticks a burger in a bun, no onions, one tiny squirt of tomato sauce, wraps it in white paper and pushing it towards me, shouts, 'Who's next?' as he looks at the queue behind me.

'You not getting one for Sorrel?' Claudia asks, glancing over her shoulder at Brian as she walks across the playground whilst suggestively biting into her burger.

'Didn't you notice? She's not in today.' Luce dips her hands into the bag of cheese and onion crisps she'd bought, which Brian had thrown over the top of the fence, crisps not being able to be pushed through without turning into dust. 'I sent her a text but she's not answered.'

I hadn't got a text from Sorrel either, and when I'd tried to phone her to find out why she wasn't on the bus, her phone had just gone straight to voicemail.

We huddle on the corner near the science block, everyone but Claudia trying to keep the wind from flipping our skirts up around our waists.

'It's not like her not to tell us if she's not going to be in,' I say, eating my burger whilst keeping my legs crossed to clamp my skirt between my thighs. 'She's been bunking off a bit recently.'

166

'She's been, like, dead moody too,' Tammy Two-Names says. 'She's always, like, snapping at everyone.'

'She might be a preg-head,' Nat says. 'My mum was always snapping when she found out she was preggers.'

'That's because it wasn't your dad's baby she was carrying,' Claudia points out. 'It belonged to the guy who came to read the gas meter.'

'S'pose,' Butterface says, getting out her handbag mirror and peering at her yellow greasy face.

She's probably overdoing it with the Maybelline today because we've got a double period with our hot geography teacher, Jon 'Buff' Butler, next, and whilst we all think he's a golden-haired Lurve God, Nat has the *serious* hots for him.

'Sorrel's defo not preggers,' I say. 'Nothing happened with Warren other than sharing the odd burger. I'll send her another text and if she doesn't answer by the time I've finished my Big B, I'll hunt down Jas and see what's up.'

'He has become, like, *so* cute,' Tam says, nudging me as FB walks towards us. 'Hi, Frazer!' she pouts as he gets level with us.

Tits Out and Butterface giggle as Tam licks her lips, pretending it's to do with the burger. 'You OK?'

So that I don't look like I'm crossing my legs because I need the loo, I unclamp my thighs just as a gust of wind shoots along and sends my skirt round my waist. Even a flash of meaty upper thigh doesn't have FB looking at me.

'Fine, thanks,' he says, smiling at all of us, before walking on towards the library, a pile of books under one arm, his rucksack slung over his shoulder.

It's been over two weeks since the fight in English, and a week since FB got back from his exclusion. Every day he was away I thought about trying to contact him, slipping out of the house at midnight and throwing stones up to his bedroom window, but decided against it when I realized I don't actually know which window is his, and it would be just my luck to wake his parents, or worse, lob a stone right through the glass, smash it and possibly injure someone. So I thought I would wait until he came back to school before trying a grovelling apology, but when he returned, *everything* had changed.

It's amazing what beating up the school bully right under a teacher's nose does for your street-cred. FB has gone from being the nerdy freaky Beakster to the boy that took on Pinhead and not only won, but also now has Pinhead telling everyone FB deserves respect.

Unfortunately, whilst everyone has been talking about FB, FB still won't talk to me. I've tried to go up to him but he either blanks me, walks away, talks to someone else, puts his head in a book, in other words, *anything* rather than speak to me. Once, I thought I'd cornered him by the bike racks, but he cycled away so fast, he ran over the foot of a little kid. And I can't employ my usual technique of walking the streets dressed like a tart in a red nylon anorak because I'm grounded. I have to be home no later than five o'clock after school and no going out in the evenings or at weekends. It's no wonder life seems to be one long round of school, homework and hair washing.

'Frazer's dad is supposed to be *totally* minted,' Claudia says, watching FB. 'Swish motor and everything. First chance you get, Tam, go for it.'

'You don't, like, mind, do you?' Tam asks me. 'You and him were always, like, something.'

'It's nothing to do with me,' I say, trying not to sound sour. 'You and him do whatever you like.'

The sixth-form common room is, according to those people who've actually been in it, one of the main reasons for staying on at Burke's to do A levels. It has, allegedly, a pool table, a pinball machine, a drinks machine, a microwave, a sound system and *really* comfy chairs.

I only know all this in theory as non-sixth formers are banned from even knocking on the doors.

'Is Jasmine Callender in there?' I ask a speccy girl with short hair as she comes through the doors.

169

She looks at me, looks at Lucy and then totally ignores us, except to glare at me when I whisper, 'Spec head!' just loud enough for her to hear.

'They have it so easy, Luce!' I say, trying to peer through a tiny gap between the swing doors. 'They don't have to stand outside in the cold or hide in the cloakrooms. They can stay in the warmth and play with their balls.'

'Hello,' a deep male voice says. 'You waiting for someone?'

I turn from my gap peering to see two sixth-form boys standing next to us. One I recognize as Naz Ashri, mainly because he keeps winking, though now I know it's a nervous twitch he's lost his appeal, which is a shame as he's got the sort of dark slightly exotic looks I go for, Buff Butler and FB excepted.

'I'm Josh,' the other one says. 'I've seen you around with Claudia Barnes and her friends.'

I elbow Luce in the side, hoping that she'll remember that despite the fact Josh Caldwell is rather good-looking – tall and blond like Luce – he's a Stiff Lipper.

I glance at Naz, who's winking left, right and centre, but not at me.

'I'm mostly with Electra and Sorrel,' Luce says, clearly not wanting to be included in Claudia's tarty posse.

'Sorrel Callender? Jas Callender's sis?' Josh asks, clearly

not the slightest bit interested in *my* family tree.

'Yes, that's why we're here. We're trying to find Jasmine,' Luce says. 'Is she in there? Could you go and have a look for us?'

The two boys stand rigid. Clearly neither of them want to leave Lucy's side for a nanosecond. Eventually, after various glares are exchanged, the winker slopes off to the common room, and Stiff Lips looks at me in a *Get lost, you gooseberry* sort of way, which makes me want to stay and see him squirm.

'Me, Naz and some others are in a band,' Josh says, looking uncomfortable. 'We're playing our first gig, this Saturday the 8th. It's at the Methodist church hall on Chapel Street.' He stares at his filthy shoes. 'Um, er, you don't have to, but it would be great if you could come, but only if you want to.' Josh's head has turned the colour of a throbbing zit. 'It's quite early, six o'clock, as the church are having a Christmas pie and pea supper at eight and we couldn't get anywhere else. We could do something afterwards, maybe, if you like.'

'Well . . .' Luce looks a bit dubious, but I'm not sure whether it's because of the prospect of a date with Stiff Lips, or going to see some dodgy sixth-form band in a church hall.

'We're sort of prog rock with a touch of thrash-metal,

though Jules keeps playing Celine Dion songs. He's our rhythm guitarist, but he's only there because he's got an amp and his dad drives a van.'

'What are you called?' I ask, not because I'm interested, but so that Josh remembers I'm still standing next to him.

'The Dogs of Doom, you know, after a line in one of Led Zeppelin's songs? We were called The Dog's Bollocks but the church wouldn't let us use the hall with that name.'

Luce is *so* not a metal head. She doesn't even like it when Justin Timberlake gets a bit shouty.

'Naz is on drums and I'm on vocals,' Josh says. 'Then there's Spooner on lead guitar, Tegs on bass and, like I said, Jules on rhythm.'

I'm just wondering how Stiff Lips manages to sing properly if his mouth is paralysed, when Naz appears with Jas. Given she's at school she's wearing an amazing amount of lip gloss.

'Oh, it's you,' she says with a sneer. 'What?'

'Is Sorrel ill?' I ask. 'She's not at school and she's ignoring her phone.'

'How should I know?' Jas says, pouting and smoothing down her already poker-straight black hair.

'Because she's your sister,' Lucy chips in, quite sharply for her. 'You share a bedroom, remember?'

'Well, she was fine this morning,' Jas says. 'Had breakfast in school uniform and everything. That's all I know.'

'Well, she never turned up,' I say. 'We're worried.'

'So will she be if Mum finds out she's bunking,' Jas says, before turning and taking her pert bum to the land of the pool table.

'Cow!' I mutter. 'Luce, ring your mum and ask her not to pick you up, and then let's go round after school and see if she's OK. If we go straight there and back, I can still be home before the five o'clock curfew.'

'So,' Josh Caldwell says to Luce. 'Will you be there on Saturday?'

Lucy fiddles with the ends of her hair. I expect Stiff Lips thinks she's being all coy, but I know Luce, she's a bit nervous and can't decide what to do. I'm thinking, *He's a sixth former, he's not a minger and he's in a band.* If you ignore the stiff lips slur, what's there to say *no* to?

Josh is going very red and I can see beads of sweat form on his forehead.

'It's for a charity. The British Heart Foundation. My dad died of heart failure last April.'

Back of the net, Josh! I know that with the death and charity angle, he's caught Luce hook, line and sinker.

'Oh that's terrible,' Lucy gushes. 'Your poor dad, I

173

mean, he's dead now, so more poor you. I'll be there and get everyone I know to come and support you.'

'Do you really think his dad's heart conked out?' I say as we head to Buff-lusting.

'If he didn't, why would he say it?' Luce asks. She's texting James to tell him to invite all his friends from King William's, but she's trying to do it with her phone still in her bag so the teachers won't see.

'Duh, the sympathy vote,' I say. 'You weren't going to go out with him until he played the death card.'

'That is *so* shallow, even for you!' Luce says, looking genuinely shocked and even I wonder if I've gone too far.

'Soz,' I say. 'It's just I can't believe you've got a date, just like that! I never get a date and you got one without even trying.'

'I really thought you and Frazer would end up together,' Lucy says as we walk just quickly enough to geography that we're there in time, but not so quickly we're sweaty and stinky for Buff. 'It seems such a shame.'

'You heard Tam, she's going to ask him out,' I say. 'I've missed the FB boat and it's all my own fault.'

'Why don't I invite him to Josh's gig on Saturday?' Luce suggests. 'As it's for charity, asking him would be legit.'

'And that would help me how?' I say. 'Don't forget,

while you're off with the lead singer being a teenage groupie, I'll be at home under armed guard.'

It's Phil's Christmas work do on Saturday night, a regional gathering of the mobile grease monkeys, so whilst I stay in my room, old Mrs Skinner from next door is employed to sit on our sofa, guzzle biscuits and make sure I don't abscond.

'You've got to come!' Luce gasps. 'I can't go on my own. Can't you pretend it's a carol concert or something and they'll let you out?'

'Nice try, Luce, but I don't think the thought of "Away in a Manger" rather than "Whole Lotta Love" is going to change their minds,' I say. 'Mum would probably worry that somehow I'd get hold of a church candle, burn the place down and still claim it wasn't my fault. Anyway, Sorrel will come with you.'

'I doubt it,' Lucy says sadly. 'I don't know what's up with her, but as a friend, Sorrel seems to be slipping away from us.'

Chapter Fourteen

We hardly ever go to Sorrel's. Even Sorrel doesn't like her own house.

She shares a bedroom with bitchy Jas, it's usually full of snotty kids, reeks of cabbage and lentils and the loo doesn't flush properly as Yolanda's on a save-water kick and has put a brick in the cistern. The brick theory is you don't use as much water when you flush, which is fine for your everyday pee, but for anything more substantial you can stand in their bathroom yanking the handle over and over again. This not only rather defeats the aim of trying to save water, but is also time-consuming and excruciatingly embarrassing when someone's waiting outside.

So before we leave school after final reg, Luce and I go to the loo, *then* get on the bus, stay on for another five stops after my usual one, get off on Southwood Lane and wind through the side streets to number 5 Forge Road, the row of modern terraced houses where the Callenders live.

Yolanda hasn't got round to converting the Goth stretch-limo she's bought to run on vegetable oil, so it's just sitting on the drive as if inside the house, people are waiting to go to a funeral. And talking of dead, most of the plants in pots dotted around the tarmac have snuffed it either because they've frozen to death, or been sat on, peed on or dug up by the family's black and white moggy, Parsley.

As there's no longer an electricity-draining bell, just an enormous lump of wood on a piece of string tied to the inside of the letterbox, I pick up the wood, fret about possible splinters and hammer on the door.

I can hear movement in the house, footsteps along the hall, and then the door opens.

'Oh. My. God!' I'm *totally* gobsmacked. 'Look at you!'

Luce juts her head over my right shoulder, gasping lunchtime's cheese-and-onion-crisp breath in my ear at the sight of Sorrel.

Our bezzie is wearing spray-on tight black trousers, a low-cut yellow top, massive gold hoops in her ears and what must be practically an entire tube of shimmery gloss on her lips. But the biggest shock is her hair. Usually in beaded braids, Sorrel's locks are now thick and long and glossy, and *totally* straight.

The hair + slap + tarty togs effect adds up to Sorrel looking the spitting imagine of Jasmine.

'Did you bunk off to have your hair done?' Luce asks. 'It must have taken hours.'

Sorrel casually runs her hands down the silky black curtain, clearly thrilled with her transformation. 'This?' she tosses her locks. 'Oh, I had it done last night.'

'Why didn't you say?' I ask. 'We've been texting you all day. Is your moby bust?'

The back of Sorrel's shoulders shrug as she wobbles on high black ankle boots through to the kitchen. We follow her, closing the front door behind us.

By the time we're in the kitchen, Sorrel's already sitting at the table. Luce and I join her, scraping out a couple of wooden chairs, almost certainly Yolanda-approved ethically produced pine from sustainable forests.

'I can't believe you didn't come into school to show off your new hair,' Luce says. 'It looks fab, Sorrel.'

'So, why didn't you come in?' I ask. 'You missed Luce being asked out by Claudia's ex-snog, Stiff Lips.'

'Josh Caldwell,' Luce corrects, already standing up for him. 'He's in a band called The Dogs of Doom. We're all invited to their first gig on Saturday.'

'Except I can't go as I'll never escape from Colditz,' I moan. 'Mum's out with Phil but she's shipped in a temporary prison guard to make sure I don't knot sheets together and abseil down the side of the house.'

'You *have* to come, Sorrel,' Luce says, just as I'm wondering whether the knotted sheet technique could work, or whether I'd land on the pavement in a heap with a broken leg, severe bruising and screaming in pain, a scenario that might alert The Coffin Dodger that I'd escaped. 'I'm not going on my own. What if Josh looks a dork in real life? I've only ever seen him at school. He might wear a cardigan and white slip-on shoes!' After both Pascal and Jags changed from hunks to skunks, this is entirely possible.

'Go on,' I press Sorrel. 'Why weren't you at school?'

She flicks her hair behind her shoulders. 'I had stuff to do.'

'What *stuff*?' I say, knowing full well that teenage *stuff* could mean anything from having an illegal lie-in on a school day, to doing drugs, though as Sorrel rarely takes even a paracetamol I can't imagine she'd be off school to sniff, smoke or inject anything. But she is looking *very* tarty. Could she have become a teenage prostitute and used the proceeds to pay for her new hairdo?

'Will you be in tomorrow?' Luce asks. 'Or don't you know?'

'Course I will,' Sorrel says, as if she knows for a fact that waking up on a Wednesday morning means you no longer have *stuff* to do.

'Jas knows you bunked,' I say. 'We saw her and asked if you were OK. What if she tells your mum?'

'So what?' Sorrel shrugs, examining her plum-painted nails. 'Like she cares about anything I do.'

'Sorrel, what's wrong?' Luce tries to reach over to touch Sorrel's arm but she shrinks away. 'You're not yourself.'

'Oh, who am I then?' she says sarkily. 'Beyoncé or Leona or—'

'You know full well what Luce means,' I say, rather more snappily than I meant to. 'You've been bunking off, the meat thing goes from one extreme to another and not checking your moby is abnormal. Are you still gutted about Warren and Jas?'

'Er, newsflash. There is no Warren and Jas, or Warren and anyone for that matter,' Sorrel says matter-of-factly, wagging a finger in the air.

'How do you know?' I ask.

She avoids our gaze and looks well shifty. 'You said he only had one battered sausage, and if he was seeing someone he'd defo be seeing them on a Friday night.'

180

'But that was weeks ago!' I reply. 'He could be in a two-sausage situation by now.'

A coy smile creeps across Sorrel's glossy pout, a look I haven't seen in a long time.

'He's not. I've been checking it out.' She sits back in her chair, licks her lips, and looks like a cat that's got the cream, something unlikely in a vegan household.

'Checking *what* out?' I ask having a horrible feeling I'm not going to like the answer.

Sorrel giggles, pulls her moby out from her back pocket, and shows us a grainy photo of a dark blob near a grey building. 'Him. Warren. Whether he's going out with someone or not. *That's* the stuff I've been up to.' She starts flicking through her moby, presumably looking at more undercover out-of-focus shots of the lanky louse. 'I've been hanging around Eastwood Tech after school, and the odd afternoon when I said I was at the dentist, but today I spent *all* day following him.' She sounds really pleased with herself. 'I've been to his flat too. He's defo not going out with anyone. He's never with a girl, only lads and his mum.'

'You've been stalking Warren?' I gasp. 'But I thought you hated him!'

'Only when he fancied Jas,' Sorrel says defensively. 'And he's not seeing her.'

181

'But what makes you think if he can't go out with her he'll go out with you?' Lucy shrieks.

'I'm fifteen in about ten days,' Sorrel shoots back.

'So?' I say.

She draws her knees up to her chin and hugs herself. 'So, like I'm older.'

I still don't get it, and from the looks Luce and I are exchanging, neither does she.

Sorrel rolls her eyes as if we're being stupid. 'Duh! Last time he didn't want to go out with me 'cause he said I was a kid, whereas he said Jas was hot and all woman. If he knows I'm not a kid any more . . .' She raises her eyebrows and the sentence trails off into the sort that if it were written down, would have three dots after it.

Oh. My. God.

Sorrell is thinking of dot-dot-dotting the creepy lanky louse!

'You know *why* he probably wants someone older, don't you?' I practically shriek. 'What are you going to do when he wants proof you're not a kid? What if he thinks you're really up for it?'

'Who says I'm not?' Sorrel shrugs. 'If it's good enough for Cassie Taylor.'

'Cassie Taylor's pushing a pram, you muppet!' Luce

cries. 'Claudia's seen her and says she smells of baby sick and poo!'

'*And* she's got stretch marks around her tattoo and stitches up her bum!' I add. 'She'll never hurdle for Burke's again.'

I don't actually know if this is true, but I need to throw as much anti-underage-sex ammo into this conversation as I can think of to stop Sorrel dot-dot-dotting with Warren.

It doesn't seem to have worked.

'I'm not as stupid as Cassie,' Sorrel says simply. '*I* won't get caught out.'

'Is this what this is all about?' I say, pointing at Sorrel's hair and clothes. 'You've turned yourself into Jasmine just to hook Warren?' It seems all so obvious now. 'Sorrel, you're fabulous as you are. You don't have to pretend to be someone you're not, especially your older sis!'

The back door opens and two giggling boys with cappuccino-coloured skin and pale curls race in, followed by a scrawny man with lank strawberry-blond hair scraped back into a thin ponytail. It's the twins, Sorrel's half-brothers Orris and Basil and their father, Ray Johnson. Trailing behind looking sulky and speccy is Sorrel's younger sister, Senna, a child who will never look like Jas, however much slap and straightening she tries.

'All right, girls?' Ray nods towards us. 'You staying for tea?'

Sorrel pushes her chair back. 'They were just going. Weren't you?'

It's getting dangerously close to my five o'clock curfew, so I couldn't anyway, but even if I could and fancied a mixed-bean curry or whatever's on the menu, Sorrel clearly doesn't want us here. She's already tottering back through the house to the front door, swaying her hips and jiggling her bum.

When we get to the front door I go to hug her, but she stiffens.

'What are we going to do?' I say to Luce as we walk back to the main road. 'She's about to make a terrible mistake. Even if she doesn't end up like Cassie he'll just use her and break her heart again!'

'I know.' Luce loops her arm through mine. 'But we'll be there to help her pick up the pieces.'

Chapter Fifteen

Mum is bending over my bed, her boobs and her face looming above me. I'm always slightly freaked when she does this in case the weight of The Mighty Mammaries shifts her centre of gravity and she topples over and crushes me. How tragic to be suffocated by your mother's breasts.

Her lips move, but I stay lying on my bed, my face hopefully *totally* blank, as if I've died with my eyes open and my iPod in my ears. Might serve them right if I *was* found dead on my bed. It would certainly stop them going out just as they've stopped me going out.

I've been nice and I've been nasty.

I've pleaded and I've cried.

But Mum is adamant that I'm still grounded, even though I've pointed out only total saddos or those with evil parents stay in on a Saturday night in the run-up to Christmas.

'How could we enjoy ourselves wondering what you were up to?' Mum said when I'd thrown myself on the sofa screaming about how she's ruined not just my Christmas but my life. 'Anyway, I'm surprised you feel so strongly about a carol concert. You've never shown any interest in hymns and things before.'

I'd tried the charity carol concert angle first, because even I could see that asking to go to a Dogs of Doom concert might not go down well, but my 'Think of the people who are suffering from terminal diseases!' screech didn't move Mum in the slightest. She simply said if I was so worried about not giving to charity, why didn't I donate cash out of my allowance, and if I did, she'd match my contribution with the same amount.

As clearly I'm not going to move a muscle Mum rips out one of my earplugs, which I think counts as parental assault.

'As I was saying,' she says. 'Mrs Skinner is already downstairs and Jack is having a sandwich.'

I continue the dead-on-the-bed look.

'I didn't make you one because you said you weren't hungry.'

I did, but that was only for effect. I'm starving.

'We should be home about midnight, and Mrs Skinner won't go until we're back, OK?'

This is clearly a warning that I'll be under The Coffin Dodger's watch at all times, just in case I'm tempted to slip out of the house and ramraid the nearest Tesco, or whatever it is they're worried I'm going to do when they're not around.

Mum looks at her watch and I look at her dress. She's wearing some vast grey shapeless thing that I haven't seen since she was at her porkiest, but she's wound lots of fake pearls around her neck so she looks sort of glam in a grey-tent-and-cheap-beads type of way.

'Drinks are from six and it's going to take us a good hour and a half's drive to get there so we'd better be off,' she says. 'I expect you'll be in bed by the time we're back, so see you in the morning.'

She bends over to give me a kiss, and although I'm mad with her and still a bit concerned she'll topple over, I reach up and give her a hug. If her and Phil got mashed up on the motorway, I'd never forgive myself for blanking her the last time we were together.

As she leaves, I ram my earplugs in and flop back on my pillows.

I don't just want to go to the gig because everyone else is going and I'll be a social leper on Monday morning if I don't.

I *have* to go.

Luce rang this afternoon to say she'd been at Eastwood Circle this morning to buy a new top for this evening, and she'd seen FB. I was surprised that FB was in Top Shop, but it turned out she also went to a bookshop to look up stuff about Led Zeppelin so she could be all knowledgeable in front of Josh, and whilst she was there she saw FB crouched on the floor in the reference section.

'When I saw him I told him that Tamara was going to ask him out and that if she did and he said *yes*, you'd be gutted and that your Christmas would be ruined,' Luce had said.

'You didn't!' I'd shrieked, knowing full well that she had, and sort of glad that she did.

'And then I said you'd be at the gig tonight and he should come along too, and he said he'd think about it.'

'But Luce I can't go!' I'd shrieked again. 'I'm locked up! If he thinks I've stood him up, this will just make things worse. You've got to tell him that I'm grounded until at least Christmas because I have an evil mother!'

'Your mum's lovely and *you've* got to find a way to get out tonight,' Lucy had said simply.

And she's right. I do.

Mrs Skinner looks up from her *Puzzler* magazine as I come into the kitchen.

'Was that you in the garden, Electra?' she says. 'In your nightwear? It's a bit early to be going to bed.'

'I've got a headache,' I say, horrified to see that the relic has taken her false teeth out and put them on the arm of the sofa. She must be just sucking the chocolate Boasters with her gums. 'I just went out to see if some air might help, but it didn't. I think it might be a migraine.'

'Have you taken anything?' she asks.

'Yes.' I put on my most whiney voice. 'But it won't shift. I might just go and lie down in the dark for a few hours to see if it'll help.' I hang my head and cover my eyes as if the kitchen light is too bright, keeping my shoulders hunched in case The Coffin Dodger sees I've got the air bra on under my nightwear.

The relic makes sucking noises with her gums. 'My Frank used to get terrible migraines when he worked for the council, but only at weekends. Used to spend the entire time in the dark with a cold flannel on his head.'

I suspect that Mr Skinner only had weekend headaches because without work he was around his wife and her constant yakking the entire time.

'Let me know if you need anything,' Mrs S shouts as I go upstairs.

Then I stand outside my bedroom door, close it with a

bang, and creep back down, through the back door and out into the garden.

Moments before, when Mrs S thought I was outside having a gulp of migraine-busting air I was actually stuffing some clothes, my bus pass, my moby and some money behind a holly bush in the garden. My original plan had been to get rid of the PJs in the garden, but it's too cold to start stripping off, plus it will make changing back into them much easier, so I keep them on and wriggle into jeans and a black polo-neck, slip on trainers and brush garden debris off my legs. At least I *hope* it's garden debris. I've only got the light of the moon and my moby to guide me, so it's difficult to see just what sort of organic matter might be smeared on my clothes. I wouldn't put it past Tiny, the Skinners' mega-moggy, to leave a dirty protest on my stuff as revenge for Dad constantly chasing it out of the garden when he lived here.

I slip round the side of the house, through the side gate, lock it, push the key on a string back under the gate, and head out into the street and towards the bus stop. I'll be back by eight at the latest. I'll ditch the clothes in the garden and wander back into the kitchen in my PJs as if I've had a good kip and my migraine has gone. If Mrs Skinner puts her head round my bedroom door she'll think I'm sleeping. As I left my room, even *I* thought the row of pillows down the centre of my bed looked like me. A rather wide squashy sausage.

Lucy is standing outside the church hall with Sorrel, who's in full Warren-baiting gear.

When she went back to school *everyone* said how like her sister she looks. Even Mum got Sorrel and Jasmine mixed up. When I got home on Tuesday (one minute before the start of curfew), Mum – who'd been at Eastwood on one of her college days – said she'd seen Jasmine hanging around the Tech and hadn't realized she'd left our sixth form. I didn't squeal on Sorrel. I just said I didn't know what was going on, which is the truth. Sorrel's not said a word about Warren or dot-dot-dotting since we were in her house, and both Luce and I are a bit afraid of bringing the subject up and reminding her of what she intends to do.

Luce jumps up and down waving when she sees me.

'You're late!' Sorrel says. 'We thought you weren't coming.'

'I made a detour for some chips,' I say. 'I was starving.'

'How did you get out?' Lucy squeals, hugging me. 'I wasn't sure if you could do it.'

'I launched one of my famous plans,' I say. 'Operation

191

Holly. I hid some clothes behind a bush in the garden and slipped out. I'm not here. You haven't seen me. I'm a ghost. The real me is in bed with a migraine.'

'I've been helping Josh set up,' Luce says excitedly. 'I've been carrying wires and everything!'

Clearly Luce is enjoying her role as teenage groupie, and I have to admit I feel a touch smug as she leads me and Sorrel to the front of the queue and says to the boys on the door (neither of whom are even last-on-the-planet-fanciable), 'We're with Josh,' and the boys nod and let us push past the trestle table.

'As it's for charity, shouldn't we pay or something?' I ask, as the non-fanciables rip raffle-ticket type numbers out of a book and take money from people clearly not cool enough to know anyone in the band.

'You can give a donation later,' Luce says. 'Look, there's Josh!'

We push through the crowd to the front of the hall.

On the small stage, Josh, wearing *very* tight black jeans, a black and silver Led Zeppelin T-shirt and a wide studded belt, is yelling, 'One. Two. One. Two,' into a microphone.

'A sixth former and he can't count up to three,' Sorrel says in mock sarcasm.

Lucy scrambles up the steps at the side of the hall to

speak to Josh, and I turn and scan the growing crowd for any sign of FB.

'Hiya!' Claudia Barnes appears next to me, presumably having stuck her tits out and pushed her way through the crowd. 'I saw Lucy so thought you'd be near.'

'Anyone else here?' I say, wondering if she'd seen FB on her way through the crowd and might mention it.

'Loadsa people,' she says. 'By the way, I've seen Jags and told him that I still owe you a date. He's well up for it!'

I'm shocked.

I'd *totally* forgotten about the greasy munchkin.

'You've set me up on a date with Jags?' I shout above the noise. 'That bet was weeks ago!'

'So, you still won!' Claudia yells back. 'He didn't realize who you were but I pointed you out.'

'Claudia!' I screech, grabbing her arm. 'I've gone off him!'

I *so* don't fancy the little greaseball, although I'm mega-miffed he didn't realize who I was.

'Gotta go!' Claudia screeches back. 'Nat's around somewhere and if James Malone has brought that QB bitch, Fritha Kennedy, it might all kick off.'

I let her go as Natalie still hasn't forgiven James Malone for binning her for a QB girl, and a girl-brawl at a charity night probably isn't a good idea.

Lucy comes down the stairs and pushes her way to join us.

'They'll be on any minute,' she gasps. 'Josh is dead nervous.' Her button nose wrinkles. 'Urgh. What's that smell?'

'I think it's cat pee,' I say. There's been a bit of a whiff coming up from my jumper and it doesn't smell like damp soil.

A boy with longish greasy hair bounds on to the stage.

'Let's give it up for The Dogs of Dooooooooom!' he yells as five lads bound on to the stage and the crowd goes wild.

Unfortunately, the band's grand entrance is rather spoilt by Greasy Hair tripping over a wire on his way off the stage, and some ear-splitting feedback as The Dogs of Doom pick up their instruments.

As six coloured lights in a box at the side of the stage flash on and off giving the atmos more of a disco feel than a rock concert, Josh starts screaming something unintelligible into his microphone and jumps around the stage as if he's caught his bits between the guitar strings and is receiving multiple electric shocks.

Lucy seems impressed, though. She's beaming and clearly fancies the tight jeans off Josh, who even I can see is very good-looking and clearly doesn't have stiff lips if the swallowing of the microphone is anything to go by.

There are more screaming songs that I can't make out, a rather odd guitar solo that sounds suspiciously like a tribute to Celine Dion from a lad with bright-red hair, round glasses and a purple flowery shirt, but still no sign of FB. It's probably just as well, the way I'm looking and smelling. It's hot in here but I can't take my jumper off or people will see I've got my tartan PJs on, but as I heat up there is an overwhelming smell of cat pee, which, mixed with the smell of sweaty armpits around me, is almost toxic.

Then, at last, the screaming songs stop, Josh lays his guitar on the floor, walks to the front of the stage and sits on the edge, his spidery long legs dangling over the side. Everyone can see from his face that he has something serious to say and the crowd simmers down.

'The next one's especially for my dad, Jeremy Caldwell, who died of heart failure earlier this year. Love you, Dad!'

Josh looks up to the sky, or rather the cracked white ceiling of the church hall, and begins to sing 'Stairway to Heaven'. When he's not screaming or microphone swallowing, he's got a beautiful voice.

It's all very emotional.

Everyone starts swaying, tears roll down Lucy's face as she watches Josh sing for his dad, a few people hold lighters in the air, and I start worrying that the paper chains that the church playgroup have strung around the room might catch fire.

As the crowd go wild at the end of the song, Josh takes a bow and smiles right at Lucy who looks as if she might die of happiness.

But after the triumphant 'Stairway to Heaven', The Dogs of Doom start screaming again and things go rapidly downhill.

Naz seems to be playing drums to an entirely different song, and the red-haired speccy has put his guitar down and is stamping his feet, his arms folded across his chest, looking as if he might cry.

A skinny lad pushes past me, races on to the stage and then launches himself into the crowd. Then someone else joins in, and before I know it I've found myself at the front of a mini-mosh pit with people landing on me and lads smelling of BO, fags and cheap booze being passed over my head. The church hall has probably never seen anything like it, and I can't imagine the pie and pea Christmas supper is going to get off to a prompt start.

'I've had enough,' I yell at Sorrel, as someone else lands on my shoulder and she shoves them off, sending them tumbling to the floor. 'Do you want to go?'

Sorrel nods, but Lucy motions that she's going to stay put and will ring us.

As we push our way through jumping bodies, there's no sign of FB, but I do spot Jags. He's at the back, leaning against a wall, running his hands through his over-gelled hair.

At one time, the sight of him would have set my heart racing, my knees trembling, and my stomach churning, but now, as far as Jags-lust is concerned, my body feels completely numb.

As I pass by him, he shouts something at me and I feel his breath on my cheek.

'What?' I yell back over the noise.

Jags steps forward and cupping his hands around his mouth shouts into my left ear, 'Claudia Barnes tells me I'm your prize.'

I look at him, small and greasy and loving himself, and think, *How could I ever have fancied this oily little munchkin?* How could I have wasted all that time working out ways of getting close to him, tarting myself up, hanging around the sports centre, learning Shakespeare, just in the faint hope he'd notice me. I've spent hours writing my name next to his, planning what engagement ring he was going to give me, dreaming of running hand in hand through a corn field or frolicking in the surf, him looking gorgeous, me with golden spaghetti limbs, not fat mottled salami ones.

But now, like Lucy and Pascal, I can't imagine what I ever saw in him.

'Some prize!' I shout back, as I see Sorrel still pushing her way out ahead of me.

'But Claudia said you fancied me,' he bellows. 'You saying you don't?'

'Can you blame me?' I yell. 'You never knew my name. You ignored me. When you did speak to me, you treated me like a pile of festering beetle dung or called me a Swamp Monster. Yeah, like I really fancy you now!'

Ooh, it felt good to get all that out. Jags can go and find some other kid with a crush to ignore and humiliate.

I'm about to follow Sorrel but find that someone has grabbed my wrist firmly and is pulling me back.

Jags.

I don't know whether he drags me towards him, or whether the crowd pushes us together, but I'm nose-to-nose with Jags and he's still holding on to my wrist, a little too firmly for comfort.

'You're a Greek Goddess when you're angry, do you know that?' he says into my ear, and then plants his lips on mine and snogs my face off.

Until recently, if anyone had told me The Spanish

Lurve God would call me a Greek Goddess and give me a passionate snog despite my smelling like a cat litter tray and having chip-breath, I would have put a year's allowance on my knees going weak, possibly actually fainting and coming round at his feet, drooling and dazed as fireworks went off all around me. But as his tongue explores my molars, all I can think of is:

HE'S A PLUNGE PUCKER!

Yes! The Spanish Lurve God kisses like he's unblocking a drain, and what with the smell of body odour all around me and cat wee up my nostrils, I really feel as if I'm involved in the sort of sewage removal my father's firm, Plunge It Plumbing Services, deals with. So instead of fireworks going off in my head, I have an image of my father driving his plumber's van with a big plunger painted down the side.

As Jags shows no sign of coming up for air and, quite frankly, I'm bored, I pull away from him. He lunges in for another throat unblocking, but I wriggle free and wrench my wrist from his hand. Finally the strong salami limbs have come in useful! A spaghetti-wristed girl might still be attached to Jags whether she wanted to be or not.

'What the hell do you think you're doing?' I snap, wiping my mouth with the back of my hand, which I hope is totally humiliating for him. 'Drop dead, munchkin boy!'

Sorrel's leaning against the wall outside. It's a clear cold night and she's blowing hot-breath rings into the freezing air as if she's pretending to smoke.

'What happened to you?' she says when she sees me all flustered and breathless, not from my Jags encounter but from pushing my way through the sweaty throng.

'I've just been snogging Jags,' I say casually, and wait for the reaction as we weave our way back to the main road.

'Jags, Jags?' Sorrel gasps. 'You've finally snogged The Spanish Lurve God?'

'Slough Sleaze Bag more like. He just grabbed me and went for it. It went on for ages and was gross. I can't think what I ever saw in him.'

Sorrel makes a face. 'Did Tits Out set you up?'

'Yeah, but when I told him I no longer fancied him he just pounced on me. All that time tarting myself up, and now I find out he goes for daggy girls who wear jammies under their clothes and smell like a cat's bum!'

Sorrel giggles. 'Look, everyone's out tonight,' she says. 'Fancy getting some cans and crisps and going back to mine for a Jags snog de-briefing?'

I look at my watch. Not yet seven. As long as I'm back

by eight, my migraine cover should be fine, and even going to Sorrel's is better than being with The Coffin Dodger and her free-range gnashers. Plus, I can't leave Sorrel on her own looking like Jasmine. What if she bumps into Warren?

'So, where is everyone?' I say, as we sidle past the Goth limo and head up the drive. The house is in darkness, other than a few solar lights in plant pots by the front door, which, because it's December and gloomy practically all the time, barely glow.

'Ray, Mum, the twins and Senna are at a panto.' Sorrel tries to put her key in the lock, but as it's dark it takes several attempts. 'Jas is out with some other Saturday girls from New Look.'

We get into the house, Sorrel switches on the hall light and then we hear it. A sort of low grunting sound. She quietly puts down the Coke and crisps we bought moments earlier, and cocks her head, listening to the noise.

It seems to be coming from upstairs, directly over the hall.

'Unless there's a pig trapped on your landing you've got burglars!' I whisper as Sorrel starts tiptoeing up the stairs.

Even though I'm freaked, I follow her, picking up a Diet Coke can as something to lob in case it is a burglar, although it occurs to me that there's very little a thief would want here unless they're into seed-sprouting jars or yoghurt makers.

Moonlight is streaming through the landing window so that the upstairs corridor is bathed in a gloomy eerie glow.

The piggy grunts seem to be coming from Jasmine and Sorrel's room. The bedroom door is half open, and as Sorrel peers round it, I peer over her shoulder.

And then we see what's making the noise.

It's not a burglar huffing and puffing, or a pig with its snout trapped in a bag.

On the bottom of the bunk bed are two figures and, by moonlight, we can just about see who they are.

Jasmine and Warren are making out in Sorrel's bedroom.

Sorrel slumps against the bonnet of the Gothmobile. From the gasping noises she's making and the way she's holding her stomach, I think she might be about to be sick.

Oh, gross. I was right. She *has* been sick. Right by the front left tyre.

'Sorrel, I'm so sorry.' I hug her, but she breaks free to chunder again, this time by the front right tyre. I'm just relieved that I haven't got any Sorrel-vomit on me, as I don't think the jumper would survive a BO/cat pee/barf combination without disintegrating. 'I don't think they saw us.'

'Of course they didn't see us,' Sorrel snaps. 'They had other things on their mind, didn't they?' She begins to heave again. 'Let's get out of here.'

Chapter Sixteen

It's late.

Very late.

I only realize just how late when I hear Mum and Phil come in and glance at the clock.

Gone one.

I think Phil must have had a bit to drink, as his voice is loud. I can hear him standing in the hall thanking The Coffin Dodger for being such a good prison guard.

Yeah, right.

Although I've been in bed for ages, I haven't slept. My brain is so buzzed I'm seriously freaked it's going to short-circuit and go into some sort of neurone overload causing massive sparking at the synapses, at which point I'll either die, or become a dribbling vegetable, perhaps an aubergine.

After Sorrel and The Slaggy Sister Incident the two of

us walked round and round the streets. Sorrel didn't say anything but I prattled on about the band and how long Josh and Lucy would last, whether The Slough Sleaze Bag would recognize me in daylight and not stinking of animal excrement and how I'm going to get FB to forgive me for being so shallow, in fact *anything* other than what we'd just seen and heard.

Eventually it got dangerously close to the eight o'clock curfew I'd set myself.

'Are you sure you're going to be OK?' I'd asked Sorrel as she waited with me at the bus stop on Southwood Lane. 'What are you going to do now?'

'Just wander around a bit,' she'd said. 'Then go back, go to bed and hope it's all been a bad dream.'

So before getting on the bus I'd hugged her and made her promise me she'd be OK and to ring me in the morning. Then I went home, pulled the key from under the gate, sneaked in, took off my clothes in the garden, stashed them back behind the holly bush (practically puncturing my arms from the prickly leaves), and appeared in the kitchen, migraine miraculously gone, and woke up a snoring Mrs S by raiding the fridge.

I took a cheese and pickle sandwich on white to my room, wondered how I was ever going to get two images out of my mind, one, Jags lunging at me and the other,

Warren Cumberbatch's moonlit bum, read an *I'm in love* text from Luce, who was out with Josh and the band having a kebab, and congratulated myself on the sneaky way I'd managed to outfox Phil, Mum and The Coffin Dodger, and creep out of the house and back without being noticed.

My bedroom door opens quietly and light streams in.

'Mum?' I whisper into the dark. If it's not a family member coming into my room in the early hours of Sunday morning I could be in serious trouble.

Luckily for me, it is.

'You still awake?' Mum asks, coming in and sitting on the end of my bed.

'Sort of,' I say, shuffling up the mattress. 'Did you have a nice time?'

'Not really,' she laughs. 'I'd forgotten what it's like to be a designated driver and stone-cold sober whilst everyone else is getting merry.'

'You should have stayed over, then you could have had a drink,' I say, knowing how much Mum likes a glass or three of red wine.

'Best not.' She squeezes my toes over the duvet. 'Mrs Skinner says you had a migraine and were in bed most of the time. You OK now?'

'It was just a headache,' I say. 'Nothing major.'

'Well, try and get some sleep.'

She kisses me on the forehead and I circle my arms around her neck. I *so* want to talk about what's happened. The Browns have never been a *Let's sit down and talk about it* sort of family but, after Dad left, Mum and I made a pact that we'd try and talk to each other more. But there are some things that are best left unsaid, especially if they involve going AWOL, changing into pee-stained clothes, being snogged by a greasy munchkin, and then seeing your best friend's sister at it in a bunk bed with an ex-burger flipper.

'Electra?'

Someone's calling me.

Is it Jags pleading with me to reconsider my feelings towards him, trying to convince me he's really a lush-lipped Spanish Lurve God, not a plunge-pucker Slough Sleaze Bag?

Is it FB telling me he's forgiven me for being so shallow and asking me out?

Maybe it's Sorrel about to confess that she's murdered both Jas and Warren, and they're now lying fatally injured on the bottom bunk.

'Electra?'

It's Mum.

I look at the clock. Just before two. Despite my stressy head, I must have nodded off after all.

'Yolanda Callender's on the phone,' Mum whispers. 'Sorrel's gone missing. When did you last see her?'

At first I fibbed and said that I hadn't seen Sorrel since school on Friday, but then I began to freak that Sorrel might be in real danger, that she'd been abducted from the bus stop by aliens in a spaceship, or, more likely, perves in a car. So after Mum went downstairs to speak to Yolanda, I raced after her and spilt some of the truth, which is that I'd seen Sorrel at the bus stop, but not that we'd been to the concert, and certainly not The Slutty Sister Incident.

Mum didn't have a go at me for pulling a fast one on The Coffin Dodger, she just phoned Yolanda straight back whilst I started marching around the kitchen, partly to keep warm and partly to try and stop myself from having a mega-panic attack about the trouble we're in.

'You've got some explaining to do later, young lady,' Mum growls. The use of the phrase *young lady* coupled with the menacing voice leaves me in no doubt that I am almost certainly going to be grounded for a year once this is all over.

It's been about fifteen minutes since Mum phoned Yolanda, and we're both downstairs, waiting for her to arrive. Mum's sitting on the sofa wrapped in her grey fleecy dressing gown, icy disapproval blasting from every pore as I do another panicky circuit of the kitchen table.

Above us, the doorbell goes, and we troop upstairs. Whilst I hover in the hall, Mum ushers an ashen-faced Yolanda into our front room where she sits huddled in a thick brown coat, her braids cascading over a brightly coloured scarf wound tightly around her head. The scarf is the only cheerful thing in the room at nearly two-thirty in the morning.

'Pop the heating on will you, love?' she says to Phil. He's appeared at the door, bleary eyed, wearing a pair of boxer shorts and a sweatshirt, reeking of alcohol. 'Coffee, Yolanda?' Mum offers, as Phil leaves us.

'No, thank you, Ellie.' Sorrel's mum shakes her head.

'Have you phoned the police?' Mum asks, moving a pile of papers and magazines from the sofa bed and gesturing to Yolanda to sit down as I perch on the arm with my moby and try to phone Sorrel again.

Yolanda sees me. 'If you're trying to call Sorrel, her phone is still in the house. We have phoned the police but they've said it's very common for teenagers to stay out for a night, but that if she doesn't turn up tomorrow to phone them again.'

'You must be worried sick,' Mum says as the heating comes on, the pipes banging and clattering beneath the floorboards.

Yolanda fixes her dark anxious eyes on me. 'Electra. Your ma says you saw Sorrel at the bus stop. Which one and when?'

'The one near yours,' I say. 'On Southwood Lane. About seven-thirty.'

'And she was fine then?' Yolanda asks. 'She seemed happy, for Sorrel?'

'Well . . .'

'What had you been doing before that?' Mum asks.

'Just stuff.' I start examining the tartan pattern on my PJs. Only a few hours earlier I'd been wearing them to the gig, snogging Jags in them. I've a horrible feeling the cotton may have absorbed some of the cat-pee smell, which serves me right for getting back into bed without changing them.

'What sort of *stuff*?' Mum's voice is sharp.

I realize that I've been biting the inside of my cheek so hard I can taste blood in my mouth.

'We went to this thing—'

'The carol concert?' Mum interrupts.

'It wasn't a carol concert. It was a gig by some sixth-form boys at our school. Lucy's sort of going out with the lead singer.'

'Go on,' Mum orders, and I know I've got zero choice but to tell the truth, even if it gets me grounded for *life*.

'Me and Sorrel left early 'cause people started moshing, you know, jumping into the crowd? So we got crisps and stuff and went back to hers – yours – on the bus.'

'And what happened there?' Yolanda asks.

I don't say anything, just stare at my tartan legs and feel sweaty with fear.

'Sorrel left her bag and telephone in the hall,' Yolanda says. 'And crisps. Something made her leave the house in a hurry. Now, what was it?'

I think of Warren's bum and feel sick.

'Electra, for goodness' sake this is important!' Mum snaps. 'The stuff about you sneaking out of the house we'll deal with later. I'm only interested in helping Yolanda get to the bottom of what's happened to her daughter. Now stop playing stupid games and tell us if something's happened we should know about.'

I swallow hard. It feels as if a golf ball is lodged in my throat.

Here goes.

'We walked in on Jas and this lad called Warren

Cumberbatch. Whilst you were out, they were doing it in Jas and Sorrel's bedroom.' Jas is never going to let me use her New Look staff discount now. 'At least, that's what it looked like.'

'Jasmine never mentioned Sorrel coming back,' Yolanda says, not batting an eyelid that her eldest daughter has been caught making out on a bunk bed.

'They didn't see us. We ran out 'cause Sorrel was dead upset. She's had a thing for Warren for ages.'

'Is that Burger Boy?' Mum asks and I nod.

'She thought he fancied her, but he fancied Jas, but Sorrel thought she was in with a chance if she looked more like Jas.'

'So she was upset when she saw them together?' Yolanda asks.

I nod. 'She freaked and vommed on the drive.'

Yolanda puts her head in her hands and begins to weep, and Mum gets up and goes over to give her a hug.

'She'll turn up, Yolanda,' Mum says, flashing me a look which says *You're dead*. 'I know she will.'

Chapter Seventeen

'We'll try again,' Dad says as I put the key in the lock and let us both into the house. 'Perhaps drive out a bit further. Maybe we should think about targeting London? What do you think?'

'Maybe,' I say, switching on the hall light and kicking off my shoes. 'I'll ask Yolanda where we should look next.'

It's been a tough week without Sorrel. I mean, I'm sure Sorrel is having it even tougher, but if she knew how upset she'd made everyone, especially her friends and family, I don't think she'd ever have disappeared, however much the Warren–Jas thing had freaked her.

I was sure she'd be in touch, not with her moby, of course, but perhaps ringing from a phone box. Even if she put the receiver down straight away, we'd guess it was her and at least know she was still alive. But days later there's been nothing, and now I'm freaked that what started out as one night away to get her head together has ended up with Sorrel either holed up in a drug den or, worse, dead down the bottom of a hole.

There's been a lot of tears.

Late on Sunday afternoon, the police came round and spoke to me whilst Mum was there. They wanted to know *everything*. Not just what Sorrel was wearing but who her friends are, whether she had any enemies, had met anyone on the Internet, old boyfriends, new boyfriends, any drug habits and so on. But Sorrel doesn't have any enemies or boyfriends, she's never taken drugs or run away from home before and the only thing she does on the Internet are the things we all do. But then, as Lucy once said, Sorrel has seemed to be slipping away from us recently, so perhaps there's stuff we don't know about.

That same afternoon the police went to see Lucy, but as Luce only had eyes for Josh during the gig and was at the kebab house with the band after it, she couldn't give them any new info but said she just sobbed throughout all the questioning.

On the bus on Monday morning, where the seat next to me felt heartbreakingly empty, Claudia 'Been There Done That' Barnes admitted she hadn't actually ever run away from home – she'd have to take a very big suitcase full of make-up, hair-straighteners and padded bras – but that one of her cousins, an older girl called Paula had, and apparently poor Paula had had to do all sorts of unspeakable things to get a bed for the night from strangers.

'What sort of unspeakable things?' I'd asked Tits Out, who said Cousin Paula couldn't speak about them, *that's* why they were unspeakable, but that even though she'd come home and eventually got eight GCSEs, she was never the same again, has been in and out of rehab and *still* has shockingly sunken eyes.

On Tuesday afternoon, the coppers came to the school and a policeman spoke in a special assembly appealing for information, but the word in the playground is that no one had anything new to say.

FB came up to me after the assembly and said he was sorry to hear about Sorrel, and did I know that more than a hundred thousand kids run away from home each year, but most, though not all, come home safely.

The word *most* freaked me because I wondered whether Sorrel would come into the *most* or *not all* category.

As FB ambled away down the corridor, bag slung over his shoulder, his hair even longer over his collar than I remember it in my slightly racy daydreams, it only then occurred to me that even though seconds before he was standing in front of me looking all concerned, I hadn't tried to say anything to him about the Pinhead incident, or why he didn't come to the Dogs of Doom gig after all. I wasn't thinking about fancying FB or trying to use the sympathy card to get him to ask me out. And although I *have* thought about snogging Jags, when I do, my knees don't go weak but my toes curl, so I know that I'm defo totally over him. No, all my thoughts are with my best friend who's out there somewhere, either too distressed or too dead to come home.

I really thought she'd be back today, Thursday, her birthday. Her present, a set of glitter nail polishes with topcoat and basecoat, is still wrapped and in my bedroom, my moby hasn't rung, and as Dad follows me down to the kitchen, the answerphone light isn't flashing.

'Would you like a coffee?' I ask Dad.

'Please,' he says, switching on the telly and sitting down.

Dad being allowed through the doors of 14 Mortimer Road again has been the one positive thing that seems to have come out of Sorrel's disappearance.

I'd like to say it's because the thought of Sorrel's family breaking up has brought mine closer together, but it's actually because I'm under twenty-four-hour adult watch, and as Mrs Skinner clearly can't be trusted to keep a teen-Houdini like me in, when there are no other responsible adults available Dad has been drafted in to keep an eye on me. Which is why whilst everyone else has been out putting up posters on bus stops and lamp-posts, handing out leaflets outside Eastwood Circle and the cinema or just combing the streets looking for clues in derelict buildings and park shelters, I've spent Thursday evening riding around in Dad's van staring at groups of winos and weirdos in case a pretty black teenage girl is huddled amongst them.

I'm busy clearing up coffee granules, which I've managed to scatter over the work surface, when Dad says, 'Quick! Electra! Sorrel's about to come on.'

I race over and perch on the arm of the sofa as a *terrible* picture of my best friend flashes up. When Sorrel's back she'll be nuclear-mad that they've chosen that photo. Her hair is frizzy, she's got no make-up on and she's scowling. It's the same one they've used for the police posters that are dotted all over town. It looks nothing like Sorrel, especially now she's had her hair relaxed, and I wonder whether Jas has given the police the minging photie as revenge for all the trouble her sister has caused.

'Police today appealed for a teenage runaway to contact a friend or family member to let them know she's safe.'

'Sorrel Callender, fifteen today, has been missing from

her home in Forge Road since the evening of Saturday December 8th.

'She was last seen at a bus stop on Southwood Road at approximately seven-thirty on Saturday night. She'd been out with friends, but failed to return home.

'Sorrel is black, around 5ft 6 inches tall, medium build with straight black hair. She was last seen wearing denim jeans, a black hooded jacket and black high-heeled boots.

'Her father, Desmond Callender, speaking from his home in Barbados, has made an emotional plea for his daughter's safe return.'

Standing in front of shimmering blue waters framed by palm trees, a man with a worried face comes on the screen. Other than the fact he's male, older and has magnificent fat dreadlocks like hairy sausages cascading from his head, he looks just like Sorrel.

Before he speaks, a jet ski whizzes past him in the background.

'Sorrel, everyone who loves you misses you. Whatever has gone wrong, everything can be sorted. Please get in touch to let us know you are safe and well. No one is mad at you. We just miss you and want to wish you happy birthday.'

The jet ski shoots back the other way, a water

plume rising into the air.

'Barbados looks a fabulous place,' Dad says, pressing *Mute* on the remote control to silence the local newsreader who's gone from talking about my missing best friend to a story about Santa's postbox in Eastwood Circle going up in flames, and, with it, hundreds of kids' Christmas letters. 'Has Sorrel ever been?'

I shake my head. 'I think that's part of the problemo,' I say. 'She's always missed her dad but he can't afford to come over here and Yolanda can't afford for her and the others to go over there.' I get his coffee and hand it to him. 'I thought she might have got in touch on her birthday.'

'I made all the guys take a batch of posters out,' Dad says. 'They've stuck them to their vans and asked shops to put them up.'

'Thanks,' I say, sitting next to him on the sofa, my back resting against the arm and my bare feet pushed under his thighs, not just as a sign of parental affection, but because my tootsies are cold and I can't be bothered to go to my room to get some socks. 'Dad, what if she's not back for Christmas?'

'Don't think about it yet,' he says. 'Are you away? There was talk of you going to see Vicky and Madison.' He looks round the room, which is totally unfestive despite it being December 13th. 'You normally have the tree up by now.'

I give a big sigh. 'Nothing happened about New York. Phil got the tree but it's in the garden. I don't want anything put up until we know that Sorrel is safe. It just doesn't seem right. What are you up to?' I wiggle my toes under Dad's thigh, making him flinch, probably because my toenails are freakily long.

'Nothing,' Dad says. 'I expect I'll just get one of those dinners for one and watch telly. I'll put myself on the work emergency rota this year.'

Despite the fact that all those weeks ago Dad told me that he was off women, I was sure his anti-female resolve wouldn't last long and by now he'd have found some dolly bird to kiss under the mistletoe. But there's been no mention of a replacement Candy or Caroline. According to Dad, he's just spending his days at work, and then going back to the Aldbourne Road flat on his own to microwaveable meals and sport on cable TV. He's even got rid of his bling-car, his Porsche, and gone back to driving one of the fleet vans. Jack's gutted, but being squished into the back of that thing always made me feel carsick.

I don't like to think of Dad on his own on Christmas Day. Even if Sorrel *is* back, I won't be able to enjoy Christmas, guzzling turkey and all the trimmings knowing Dad is eating his meal from a plastic tray.

'What's Nana Pat up to?' I ask. 'Can't you go to hers?'

Dad shakes his head. 'She's going up to Edinburgh to stay with your Uncle Richard and it's a long way to go to spend a day with Mum smoking and Richard lecturing her on how she's turning her lungs into one big rancid tumour.'

'But it would be better than being on your own,' I say.

'Richard's become a veggie, so it'll be some lentil roast rather than turkey.' He pulls a face, making me laugh.

'Why don't you come here?' I say. 'I could ask Mum.'

Dad roars with laughter. 'I don't think that's a good idea, do you?'

'I don't see why not. You and Mum seem to be getting on better. A few weeks ago, she'd never have even let you through the door and now you're on the sofa. Please, Dad! I'd like you to come and I know Jack would. I'm not sure about Grandma and Granddad . . .'

'The Staffords are coming?' Dad says. 'Oh, if Dorothy and William are staying they won't want me here. They didn't even want me at my own wedding!'

'That's because Mum was a teenage pregnant bride when you married her,' I remind him. 'Anyway, they're staying in a hotel and just coming for lunch. Please!'

'And what about Phil? How will he feel?' Dad asks. Mum and Dad may be getting on better, but I have no idea how Phil feels about Dad. I do know that Dad's jealous of Phil, even if he won't admit it.

'Well, if you promise to be nice to him, not call him a tattooed grease monkey or start pelting him with soggy sprouts, I don't think Phil would mind,' I say, realizing that Phil probably *would* mind but be good enough to keep quiet about it.

'Only us!' Mum calls from the hall, as Jack races downstairs and throws himself over the top of the sofa and on to Dad's lap, making Dad's thighs contract and squishing my toes.

'Look what I got!' Jack squeals, dangling a football-shaped key ring in front of Dad's face. 'I got it in the lucky dip!'

'It was his football club's Christmas do,' Mum explains, following Jack into the kitchen and flicking the kettle on. 'Five-a-side football with Santa wearing an England shirt.' She winks and everyone but Jack giggles.

'Coffee?' she asks Dad, who shakes his head, pushes Jack off his lap and gets off the sofa.

'No, thanks, Electra made me one. I'd better be getting going.' He yawns and stretches. 'By the way, we've just seen Sorrel on the news.'

'They've found her?' Mum gasps.

'No, it was a police plea,' I say. 'And her dad did a bit too, from a beach in Barbados, wishing her happy

222

birthday. I can probably find it on the Internet for you.'

'I think that's what's at the heart of all this,' Mum says, leaning against the units. 'The anger over never really getting to know her father. It's such a shame.'

'*Dad's* on his own for Christmas,' I say. '*He's* just going to have a microwaveable meal for one.'

I say this accusingly, as if Dad slaving over a hot microwave for three minutes on Christmas Day is Mum's fault, which is *so* unfair, because of course rewind almost a year, bring Candy Baxter aka The Bitch Troll into the picture, and the solo-festive microwaving is clearly all Dad's fault. Still, might as well lob the question out into the open and see whether I need to run for cover.

Here goes.

'So I thought he could come here for Christmas Day.'

Mum doesn't say anything but starts making herself a cup of tea.

'Don't worry, Ellie, I've said no,' Dad smiles to Mum's back. 'It wasn't my idea, believe me.'

'Dad, come to ours!' Jack squeals, jumping round the room like a demented frog. 'Come for Christmas! We can play on the Wii and open presents and . . . and . . .' He's breathless with excitement. 'Play on the Wii again.'

'Mum and Dad are coming,' Mum says, turning back to

the room and cupping her mug. She blows on her hot tea. 'It would be awkward.'

'Yes, Electra told me,' Dad says. 'It's fine. Honestly.'

'Perhaps you could pop over for a bit first thing on Christmas morning? Phil's on earlies and Mum and Dad aren't coming until about eleven . . .'

'I want Dad here all day!' Jack shouts. 'Phil's not our dad. Phil can go to his own family.'

The Little Runt is being useful for a change. He's doing all my pleading for me. And thinking of Sorrel without her dad, and Josh without his, has made my mind up for me.

'Well, if it's awkward here then *we'll* go to Dad's!' I say. 'We can have a meal for one together. I mean, three meals for one.'

'Can we have Pot Noodles?' Jack says jumping up and down. 'Pot Noodles and chocolate?'

I don't want to hurt Mum, but I do want to see Dad, and anyway, she'll have her mum and dad and Phil for Christmas. Our dad won't have anyone.

Mum takes a gulp of tea and Dad kisses Jack and me and heads for the kitchen door. He's just at the bottom of the stairs when Mum says, 'I'll talk things over with Phil and let you know.'

And she does, and Phil says *yes* as long as I help out

with the Christmas dinner, do all the veg and so on. So at first break on Friday I sit on a closed toilet seat in the school loos and phone Dad at work to tell him he's coming back to Mortimer Road for his Christmas dinner.

'I'll be on my best behaviour,' he says. 'There'll be no sprout-hurling, I promise.'

Chapter Eighteen

We went to London yesterday, me and Luce in Dad's van, Yolanda and her family in the Gothmobile, but we didn't see Sorrel. We handed out posters at tube stations and railway stations but no one had seen her and I don't think anyone was interested. We just got in the way of the Christmas shoppers and I knew people were thinking, 'Just another teenage runaway,' and would drop the leaflet in the nearest bin or on the pavement as soon as they thought we wouldn't notice. To be honest, I never really thought we'd find Sorrel but none of us could spend Saturday, a week to the day she disappeared, doing nothing.

'Electra! If you've got anything really dirty, can you bring it down?' Mum's bending over the washing machine and stuffing handfuls of red, white and black material in the drum. 'Jack's football kit's going in and it's filthy. I'll be doing a longer cycle.'

'I've got some rank stuff,' I say, thinking about the cat-pee denims and jumper I wore to the concert last weekend. 'I'll go and get them.'

But despite hunting high and low in my room, and even trying to sniff the stuff out by crawling around on the floor on my hands and knees, there's no sign of my stinky togs.

Then I remember. With stressing over Sorrel during the week and going up to London yesterday, I'd completely forgotten to rescue the Operation Holly clothes. They must still be in the garden, hidden in the foliage!

I go outside and peer behind the holly bush. There's no sign of the clothes. Could a fox have made off with a pair of Top Shop jeans, a black jumper and a couple of once-white trainers with a blue swoosh across them, and if so why?

Actually, the shoes are still there. I go to pick one up but it's covered in slime, and in a potential-slug induced panic, I lob it into a random laurel bush with a shriek. Damn! I can't leave trainers lurking in the garden or Mum will give me a lecture about the value of things, but I'm not going to risk getting a handful of slug slime for a pair of old Nikes.

I mooch about the garden until I find a suitable stick and then, using it, try to fish the tossed trainer out of the laurel leaves, prodding and poking as I go.

But there's more than just a slimy shoe buried in the bush.

There's a bulging black plastic sack!

My first thought is that someone has abandoned a litter of newborn kittens or puppies, but then I come to my senses and wonder why anyone would break *into* our back garden to leave a load of baby animals. But you do hear about these things and I *so* want a pupster.

I drag the bag towards me and poke it with a stick.

Nothing wriggles. Oh, what if they're dead?

Checking there are no slugs or worms hanging around, I lean over, untie the top, and, bracing myself to see something horrid, peer in. But there are no kittens or puppies, just newspapers and more rubbish sacks. I stir the contents with the stick, and notice that buried amongst the paper and plastic are an old blue towel and my jumper and jeans.

Clearly someone found my clothes, but who'd want to stash them with the other stuff? If Mum or Phil found them they'd have mentioned it, and The Little Runt wouldn't want my stuff.

So, who's been creeping about our garden pinching old clothes?

Who other than me knew about Operation Holly?

My blood runs cold as the pieces to the old clothes jigsaw suddenly fit together.

SORREL!

It's obvious! All this time we've been combing the streets looking for her, my best friend hasn't been in London, she's been dossing in our garden *literally* right under my nose.

The question is: What do I do next?

If I tell Lucy, she'll say the same as Mum will, which is that we have to tell Yolanda *immediately*. Yolanda will then telephone the police and before I know it there'll be a full-scale police operation in our back garden. If they do catch Sorrel, she'll kick and scream, and will probably run away again, maybe *never* come back. If only I could get to her first and talk to her, I'm sure I could persuade her to not only come home, but also stay home.

I look at the bag of clothes and suddenly feel desperately sad, not just because Sorrel's sleeping rough, that's bad enough, but because the one person I would normally turn to in times of trouble no longer talks to me.

FB.

Frazer's always been there when I've had a problem, not just things like being stuck on quadratic equation homework, but big things like Mum and Dad divorcing and Lucy harming herself. But I'm on my own with this one.

I push the clothes back into the bag and tuck it under the bush. Already a plan is forming in my mind.

Operation Sorrel Stake Out.

'You wimp!' I say to Jack. 'What sort of a nine-year-old doesn't want to camp outside at night?'

'Me! Now get out of my room, Poo Head!' Jack growls, holding up one of his filthy football boots in a menacing manner. I do back off, not because I'm scared of The Little Runt, but because I'm concerned he'll lunge at me with the footie boots, and I *so* don't want stud marks over my face for Christmas.

'But I'll be with you,' I say, trying to sound falsely sweet. It pains me to be nice to him but I'm desperate for a reason to sit out in the garden all night without Mum and Phil getting suspicious. 'There's nothing to be scared of. I'll sit and keep guard whilst you're asleep.'

'I'm not scared, I just don't want to camp out with you!' Jack says. 'You're no fun.'

'I could be fun,' I say. 'We could do fun things, together.'

I have no idea what fun things are to a nine-year-old boy, but I'd do *anything*, even spend the night under canvas with my brother farting toxic wind in his sleeping bag, to get Sorrel home. The idea was to persuade Jack to camp out in the garden and then whilst he was snoring, I'd be watching the side alley from the tent, ready to race out if Sorrel appeared. But, mega-annoyingly, even though Jack kept pestering everyone to sleep in the garden with him last summer, now, just because it's dark and freezing and winter and drizzling with rain, The Little Runt doesn't want to spend Sunday night under canvas with his big sister.

If Jack won't camp out, Operation Sorrel will either have to be replanned or abandoned.

Hard cash is called for.

'I'll give you a fiver,' I say. 'A fiver will buy you loads of trading cards.'

Jack thinks for a moment. I know he's thinking because his forehead is crinkling, and he's sticking his tongue through his mouth the way he does when he's concentrating on writing.

'A tenner,' I say. 'I'll give you ten pounds to camp outside with me.'

'Nah!' Jack says, sticking his tongue out, pushing past me and going downstairs.

'You're pathetic!' I say, following him. 'Do you know that? Even Theo sleeps out all night and he's tiny. You're more wimpy than a teeny-weeny rabbit.'

'If Theo could escape and open the back door he'd prefer to be inside,' Jack flashes back, heading into the front room where we keep the dinosaur family computer. '*And* he's got a fur coat.'

'Oh shut up!' I say, fed up of the increasing list of reasons why my bro and rabbit analogy hasn't worked. 'A tenner plus a fiver's worth of Pot Noodles, *and* I won't tell Mum that you've already eaten all the chocolates in the advent calendar and pushed the doors back in.'

'You did that, not me,' Jack points out.

I hear the front door open and shut, and Phil pokes his head into the room.

'All right, you two?' he says. 'What's going on?'

'Electra's trying to bribe me to sleep in the garden,' Jack says, staring at the computer screen, which is covered in little men and spaceships. 'We're up to ten pounds plus Pot Noodles.'

'Really?' Phil looks at me as I arrange my face into what I hope is a completely-blank-unable-to-read-my-mind look. 'In winter? In the cold? Now, why would she want to do that?'

There was no way out. I *had* to fess up to finding the bag of clothes and the fact I think Sorrel's been sleeping in our garden.

As I predicted, Mum immediately went into Mental Mum Mode and wanted to phone Yolanda, but both Phil and I persuaded her that until we knew for sure it *was* Sorrel, there was no point in getting anyone's hopes up, and that even if it was, Sorrel wouldn't thank us for calling the cops in. So, grudgingly, Mum agreed not to phone Yolanda but only on the promise that if Sorrel didn't come back tonight, we told the police of our suspicions and let them examine the bag. She put her foot down at letting me stay out all night on my own (the thought of which, even for Sorrel, was freaking me out) so Phil's camping out with me. I say camping, but it's more sitting on a plastic bag in the garden with a flask of soup as, after checking out the garden, Phil announced we can't use the tent as, if we pitched it where we could see Sorrel, she would see us the moment she came round the side of the house and might leg it.

I think he's forgotten that we're going to be sitting in a suburban garden watching out for my best friend, and not in the jungle stalking the enemy. He's swung into full army mode and is looking at the kitchen table where the night's supplies have been laid out. Actually, despite the seriousness of the situation, it's quite fun.

'One flask of soup, tomato?' Phil barks.

'Check.' I reply.

'One packet of biscuits, chocolate Boasters?'

'Check.'

'Bunch of Tesco carrier bags?'

'What on earth do you need carrier bags for?' Mum says. She's in her dressing gown as it's almost eleven.

'To sit on wet ground,' I say, wondering how Sorrel has managed to sleep outside for nearly a week when I'm fretting over sitting on damp grass for a few hours. I don't want piles for Christmas.

'I'm not happy about this, Phil,' Mum says. 'I still think we should have told Yolanda. If you do see Sorrel, make sure she doesn't escape.'

I wonder about the legal implications for Phil if he's caught wrestling a teenage girl to the ground, especially when we probably *should* have told Yolanda.

'Ready?' Phil asks. 'The time is twenty-three hundred hours.'

There's a light tapping on the back door, as if a tree branch is brushing against it. But there aren't any trees directly outside our back door.

I dump the carrier bags and the chocolate biscuits, rush past Mum, up the stairs to the half-landing and, after fiddling with the lock, open the door.

'I thought I'd save you the trouble of kidnapping me,' Sorrel says, stamping her feet on the ground, her hot breath rising into the cold night air. 'Can I come in? I'm freezing my bits off out here.'

I thought the first thing I'd do when I saw Sorrel again would be to shriek, throw my arms around her and laugh hysterically with joy that she was back. In fact, I burst into tears, shout for Mum and *then* hug her. I'm thrilled to see her, but with my arms round her, I can't help but notice she smells really rank, like the public loos at the bus station.

Mum and Phil must have heard the commotion as when I lead Sorrel down to the warm kitchen, Mum already has her hand on the phone.

Sorrel sees her.

'Please, Mrs B, not yet,' she pleads. 'Don't phone anyone yet. Let me have some time before the madness starts.' She looks tired, sad, dirty and *totally* defeated.

'Sorrel, your mother . . .' Mum begins, but puts the phone down. 'Half an hour,' she agrees, pulling the blue throw off the back of the sofa and handing it to Sorrel, who wraps it around herself and sinks on the sofa. 'Half an hour, and, Sorrel, it'll be all right, I promise you. Everyone will just be so relieved you're safe.'

I sit on the floor in front of Sorrel and rest my arms over her knees. I want to know *everything* that's gone on since she's been away: Where has she been? Who was she with? Was she offered drugs? But Sorrel looks too exhausted to be given the third degree. Instead, I say, 'How did you know we were going to be in the garden?'

'I saw the bag of clothes had been moved,' she says. 'Things were mixed around. I guessed you'd found them.'

'Soup?' Phil says, pouring tomato soup from the flask into a mug.

Sorrel nods and, fishing her arms from underneath the throw, takes the mug and cups it in her shaking hands. Her usually beautifully manicured nails are chipped and caked in dirt. She flashes Phil a tired smile. 'Thanks,' she almost whispers.

'So you've been sleeping right next to our house all week?' I say. 'Whilst we've been combing the streets and putting up posters, you've been here all along?'

Sorrel shakes her head and blows on the hot soup. 'Just the last two nights.'

'Where were you before that?' Mum asks.

Sorrel avoids our eyes. 'That first night, the Saturday when I didn't go back, I tried to sleep on a bench in Victoria Park, but it was too cold to stop moving, so I just ended up walking around the streets. I saw the posters, by the way. Thanks.'

'Didn't you realize how worried everyone's been when

236

you saw them?' Phil asks gently. 'What did you think was going on?'

Sorrel continues staring into her soup. 'I just thought the photo they used was minging.'

There's silence as Sorrel sips her soup and me, Mum and Phil exchange worried glances.

'So you just walked around all night?' Mum says. 'Oh, love.'

'Not all the time,' Sorrel says slightly defensively. 'Sometimes I rode the night buses, which was better 'cause on the streets tramps were always pestering us for money, and pervy weirdos wouldn't leave us alone.'

'But I thought you didn't have any money,' I say. 'You left your bag in the hall. And who were you with?'

'Keesha,' Sorrel replies. 'Keesha had some money.'

'Keesha?'

'This girl I met on the second night. She'd left her home weeks ago, but a mate gave her keys to a flat on the Northdown Estate. We'd stay out at night and go in for a nap during the day when everyone was out.'

'How did Keesha get the money?' Phil asks suspiciously.

'I dunno,' Sorrel shrugs. 'She just did.'

'But if you didn't want to go home, why didn't you come here?' I say. 'You could have stayed here, couldn't she, Mum?'

'Of course,' Mum replies. 'Anytime.'

'I just needed to get away, have a breather,' Sorrel explains. 'It was only going to be for a night, but then I met Keesha and it sort of went on.'

'And the last two nights?' I say, hugging Sorrel's knees. 'What happened to Keesha those nights? Was she here too?'

Sorrel shakes her head. 'We were in the flat during the day on Friday, but these men came back early. When they found out I'd been staying and not doing anything in return there was some sort of bust-up and someone pulled a knife and . . .' Her voice trails off for a moment. 'Keesha said it wasn't safe for me to stay there again, so I left and walked around, but I got really cold. Then I remembered the clothes you dumped and came here. I wasn't sure the stuff would still be there, but it was good that it was.' She pulls the throw tighter around her. 'When I came back tonight and saw the stuff had shifted, I knew you knew it was me, and I was just too tired, cold and hungry to keep running.'

'Sorrel, I'm going to have to ring your mum now,' Mum says gently. 'You know that, don't you?'

Sorrel nods as Mum takes the phone upstairs. We both realize Yolanda has to be told, but we also know that it'll be start of the police, and the school, and Social Services becoming involved, and for months, if not years, Sorrel's every move will be monitored and scrutinized.

I get up, take Sorrel's empty mug, and go over to the stove. Phil's opened another can of soup, chicken mulligatawny this time, and is heating it up for her. As I wait for it, I look across at Sorrel slumped on the sofa, a smelly shadow of her usual self. I can't believe that my lovely sarky, bossy, loyal friend has put herself in so much danger rather than just knock on our door.

'Should we try and phone Keesha's mum?' Phil asks. 'She'll probably be frantic with worry like we've all been. Everyone's missed you so much.'

'Keesha says she's been gone too long to go back,' Sorrel says, staring into space. 'She's never known her dad and says her mum will have probably forgotten all about her.'

Chapter Nineteen

I tiptoe along the hall with a piece of toast in my mouth and wet hair, carefully open and close the front door and head to the bus stop, carrying on the text conversation I'd started with Luce the moment I woke up and sent her the news that Sorrel was home, safe and well, and still asleep in our front room.

After Mum rang Yolanda, she cycled straight round and there was lots of hugging and crying. But even though Sorrel seemed happy to see her mum, she still refused to go home. So after a conference between the parentals in the hall whilst Sorrel and I were in the kitchen, it was agreed she could stay at ours on Sunday night and then they'd take it from there. I was all for Sorrel having my bed and blowing up an airbed for me but, as Mum pointed out, she probably needed a bath and a long sleep, and having me next to her tossing and turning on the farty airbed, probably interrogating her over what she'd been up to, not to mention setting my alarm for school, wasn't going to help. So, whilst Sorrel and Yolanda talked in the kitchen, Mum ran Sorrel a bath, and Phil and I made up the sofa bed. I propped my teddy on the pillows, and put Sorrel's birthday present and card next to him, though I expect she was too tired to open them. When she came out of the bathroom wearing one of my nighties, Mum and I practically carried her down the stairs and into the front room where she crawled into bed with Ted in her arms, so we turned out the light and left her to sleep.

There's no one else at the bus stop other than a few old codgers on their way to work.

I stand around wishing that I'd dried my hair, not because it's freezing and my head is about to turn into a block of ice, but because it's slightly windy and I'm going to end up with octopus hair, tentacles spreading out in every direction. This would be tragic on a normal day, but is double tragic on a Buff Butler lesson day, not because I'm trying to impress Buff any longer, but because geography is one of the few lessons FB and I have together. I'm hoping that after Lucy dropped hints about me being gutted if he goes out with Tam there might still be a chance for us to get together, even though he didn't turn up to Josh's concert and has practically ignored me for weeks.

Whilst Sorrel was missing I sort of forgot about things such as hair and zits, the whole FB situation and the fact that I snogged Jags and felt *nothing*, but now she's back safe and well I can feel my old shallow self returning, and I just know that my minging hair is going to stress me out all day.

I notice a poster of Sorrel taped to the bus stop and rip it off.

'Vandal,' one of the wrinklies with a briefcase mutters under his breath, just loud enough for me to hear.

'She's been found,' I say, trying to give him a sarky stare, but finding just saying the word *found* makes me smile.

'Alive?' Tits Out gasps.

I hadn't seen her approaching.

'Of course she's alive,' I say. 'Do you think I'd be beaming if she was dead?'

'Some people laugh at inappropriate times,' Claudia says. 'I knew someone who giggled all the way through his gran's funeral even though he was gutted she'd snuffed it.'

'Well, I'm laughing because I'm happy,' I say as the bus approaches. 'She turned up at our back door, late last night.'

'No!' Tits Out gasps again, and I know she'll be mega

miffed that it wasn't *her* door that Sorrel knocked on so that she could be first with the news, although when we get on to the top deck of the bus, she announces as if she's the first to know, 'Sorrel's back!'

'Is she OK?' Butterface asks as Claudia slides in next to her. I still don't have Sorrel next to me, but now the empty seat doesn't feel quite so empty.

'She's fine,' I say. 'Just a bit tired and her nails are manky. She turned up at ours last night.'

'I bet the social will be sniffing around the Callenders for ever,' Claudia says. 'Are they going to put her into care?'

'Of course not!' I say, though to be honest I've no idea what happens next.

'So where did she spend the week?' Nat asks. 'On the streets or on someone's sofa?'

'She met a girl called Keesha,' I say. Looking at Sorrel last night I got the feeling there was a lot of stuff she was keeping from us. 'Keesha seems to have looked after her. She had keys to a flat from some mates.'

'Was Keesha a prozzer?' Natalie asks. 'Were the mates scummers?'

'I bet she had to sleep with the mates to get the keys,' Claudia says knowingly. 'That Keesha girl, not Sorrel, I mean.'

I can't imagine that Sorrel would get herself into that situation, but just over a week ago I couldn't have imagined one minute we'd be giggling over me snogging Jags, and the next Sorrel would be a street rat having a knife flashed in front of her.

'So, is she on drugs?' Natalie says. 'Or preggers?'

'Neither!' I say, trying to brush my hair using my fingers. It might have been better to go to school with greasy hair rather than octopus locks. 'She's fine. Just knackered.'

'We still don't really know *why* she ran away,' Claudia says. 'She seemed fine at the gig. Razor Burns said he saw her leaving and she was OK, not upset or anything.'

'FB was at the Dogs of Doom gig?' I gasp, unable to hide my horror. 'You never said. I didn't see him.'

This is potentially devastating news. What if he saw me snog Jags? If he thinks I'll snog any passing ex-Spanish Lurve God he'll *never* ask me out.

'I thought you weren't bothered about him any more,' Claudia says. 'He was near the back with Tam. She was trying to get him to ask her out 'cause he looked really lush, all hot and sweaty.'

'Oh?' There's no way I can appear casually interested. 'And did he?'

Please say no.

Please don't tell me that they're going out.

Even though Sorrel is back and Christmas is only days away I think I might die of unhappiness.

Claudia starts brushing her hair, showering the back of the seat with bleached blonde strands.

'I think she might have come on a bit strong, you know, more or less thrown herself at him, as apparently he suddenly bolted for the door.'

'How am I going to find out whether FB saw me snog Jags?' I moan as Lucy and I leave final registration, a bit late as Mr McKay gave us a lecture about not becoming a teenage runaway and the dangers of the streets, and next time we're tempted to slam the door and walk out to remember not all missing person stories end happily.

'You could ask him,' Luce says simply, as we watch FB race out of the door.

'Oh, yeah, right. I'm really going to go up to him and say, *Did you see me snog Jags?* If he doesn't know now, he will then!'

'You could always tell him you snogged him but you didn't like it,' Luce suggests. 'You could say he was a Plunge Pucker.'

'Even worse than Stiff Lips?' I giggle, elbowing Luce in the side.

'Josh *definitely* hasn't stiff lips,' Luce smiles. 'I asked him about snogging Claudia. He said she jumped on him and he was terrified she was going to eat him.'

I can tell Luce is serious about Josh because, unlike her French fling, we haven't had all the gory details and a blow-by-blow account of every snog. There's been lots of coy looks and shy giggles but no real goss, despite me pumping her for info about what happened after the post-gig kebab.

We wander towards the bike racks where Lucy's Lurve God is bending over a bike, pumping up a front tyre, his tie loosened, his shirt sleeves rolled up, his blazer hung over the saddle.

My heart skips a beat and my stomach is filled with butterflies, not at the sight of Josh but because standing next to him is FB.

I start frantically rummaging in my bag for a pair of chandelier earrings to hook in my lobes.

'Hi, Josh,' Lucy smiles.

Josh stops pumping for a moment, looks up at her and gives a wide white grin. Luce and him make a very glam couple, sort of like the Posh and Becks of Burke's except Luce is much prettier than Mrs B and Josh doesn't have tattoos or pose in tight underwear.

My earrings are in. I smooth my hair. I'm ready to go.

'Hi,' I say, tossing my head in the hope that I'm looking glam and sparkly by the bike racks.

FB says nothing.

'What's up?' I try again.

'Someone let my tyres down and I've left my pump at home,' Josh explains, even though the question was directed at FB. Josh wipes his brow, undoes the pump and attaches it to the back wheel. 'It's probably Jules as revenge. We sacked him from the band because he wanted to play Celine Dion songs and he's really narked.'

'I thought you were dead good,' I say. 'Sorrel and I only left because the moshing got a bit much.'

I thought I'd throw that in to let FB know I left with Sorrel rather than Jags.

'Thanks!' Josh smiles, still pumping away. 'By the way, I'm glad your mate Sorrel's back safely.'

'We're going back to Electra's now, to see her,' Luce says.

'Can I ring you later?' Josh asks.

'Of course!' Lucy nudges me and grins, and I know that she is absolutely smitten with Josh, and he is with her, and I'm really happy for them both.

I'm also thrilled that Sorrel is home. If FB and I were on better terms I'd be the happiest I've been for a long time, what with term finishing on Friday, Dad coming for

Christmas lunch, and the thought of all those Christmas presents just over a week away. But even though it's supposed to be the season of goodwill and I'm tossing my hair and pouting and sticking the miracle air bra out as far as my shoulders can jerk back, FB just stands by his bike as if I don't exist.

'Thanks, mate!' Josh hands back the pump to FB who sticks it in his backpack and swings a leg over his bike.

He starts to pedal towards the school gates, and without thinking, I run after him.

'FRAZER!'

He stops and turns, and, to my relief, doesn't rush off when he sees it's me, but waits.

I catch up with him, panting. I really must do something about my fitness levels if I can't run from the bike racks to the school gate without having a heart attack. Plus, the panting sounds a bit racy, as if I'm heavy breathing.

'Claudia says you were at the Dogs of Doom gig,' I gasp. 'I didn't realize. So was I.'

'I know,' FB says, looking down and twirling one of his pedals with his foot.

'I was hoping to see you there,' I smile. 'We missed each other.'

'You were busy,' FB says coldly. 'Did you snog him for a bet too?'

Chapter Twenty

The moment Lucy sees Sorrel she throws herself at her so that Sorrel staggers back and lands on her backside on the still-open sofa bed. The sight of the two of them trying to untangle themselves from each other and the duvet is hysterical and we're all in fits of giggles, which is just as well. After FB cycled away from me and swerved into the traffic after the Jags-jibe, I could do with a laugh.

'You muppet!' Luce laughs, bopping Sorrel over the head with a pillow when they've finally stopped rolling around. 'You've had us all worried sick!'

After a bath, a good night and most-of-the-morning (according to Mum) sleep, three burgers and chips and the change of clothes that Yolanda brought over last night, Sorrel looks a bit thinner, but *much* better. She's wearing a pair of grey tracky bottoms and a black sweatshirt, and the only real evidence of a week on the streets is her nails, clean, but broken with chipped purple polish.

'Electra said a girl called Keesha looked after you,' Luce says. 'That was nice of her.'

Sorrel nods, but doesn't say anything, and for a moment the atmos is a bit tense.

'We spent all week handing out these,' Luce says brightly, sitting on the side of the sofa bed and fishing a poster from her bag. 'We put them up everywhere we could think of. You're all round town. We even went to London!'

'I saw them.' Sorrel makes a face. 'If I'd have known they were going to use that minging photie I'd have stayed at home.'

'They showed it on the news too,' Luce says. '*And* your dad made a plea for you to come back.'

Sorrel bites her lip. 'Yeah, Mrs B told me. I've seen it on your computer.' She nods towards the dinosaur sitting in the corner, its screen stuck on a news website. 'It was good to see Dad wish me happy birthday, and thanks for the pressie, E. Just what I needed!' She wiggles her manky nails in the air.

'I've got your birthday present at home,' Luce says. 'If you're not in school I'll bring it over to yours tomorrow.'

'I don't know where I'm going to be,' Sorrel says, flicking purple varnish flakes off the end of her index finger. She looks up at me. 'I know I can't stay here for ever though.'

'But you can stay for as long as you want!' I say. 'Until things are sorted.'

'*Are* things being sorted?' Luce asks. 'Are people helping you?'

Sorrel hugs one-eyed Ted to her chest. 'I've had Mum round and the police round and the social round. I've now got a case worker called Precious.' She rolls her eyes, and I get the feeling that if Sorrel had realized what trouble her running away would cause she'd have stayed at home, whatever Jas and Warren got up to on the bottom bunk. 'They've asked me to think about what I want. What I really really want.'

An ancient Spice Girls song flits into my head, and I'm *horrified* that I can be thinking of something so shallow when this is so serious.

'And?' I ask her. 'Tell me what you want, what you really really want?'

There is no hope for me.

Sorrel looks past us towards the window. The curtains aren't drawn but it's dark and rain is lashing against the windows. There's just the street light outside and the odd flash of car headlights. A typical cold and gloomy British December night.

'I want to see my dad,' Sorrel says, pulling Ted even closer. 'I want to spend Christmas with him, not here, but in Barbados, not because it's sunny or has jet skis, but so I can see how he lives and find out more about him. I feel I hardly know him.'

'Ooh, that's lovely,' Lucy gushes. 'When are you going?'

I love Luce to bits, but sometimes she can be a bit thick. She might go to a big comprehensive and mix with the likes of Butterface and Pinhead, but when she goes home at night, it's to a big house with designer furnishings and shed-loads of money in the bank. I sometimes think she forgets it's not like that for everyone.

I wait for Sorrel's sarky reply along the lines of *When I've bought my matching Louis Vuitton luggage*, but instead she says sadly, 'I'm not even going to mention it. We can't afford it, especially around Christmas when there's presents to buy and people don't go to the café as much because they're not at work, and Ray's probably going to lose his job at the camera shop after Christmas 'cause everyone is buying stuff online.'

'But if you tell your case worker—' Luce starts.

'I don't think the local council's funds stretch to sending me to Barbados for Christmas,' Sorrel says with a wry smile. 'Can't you just see the headlines? *Teenage Tearaway in Caribbean Jaunt.*'

'The council might not be able to afford it, but we can,' I say. Whilst Luce and Sorrel have been gabbing, my mind's been working overtime. 'I've got a plan.'

The girls collapse with laughter.

'No!' Luce shrieks. 'Not another famous Electra Brown plan.'

'Look at what happened with Operation Holly!' Sorrel giggles.

'Er, Operation Holly sort of brought you home,' I say. 'So don't knock my plans.'

'Go on then, what is it?' Sorrel says. 'Smuggling me on the plane as a Christmas parcel? Strapping me to the aircraft's wing and hoping I don't fall off mid-Atlantic? Or am I supposed to row across in a bathtub?'

'You could call it Operation Santa!' Luce shrieks.

My friends can hardly breathe for laughter. At least, I assume that's why they're making snorting noises as they roll around the sofa bed.

'*We're* going to raise the money for your ticket,' I say. 'Luce, do you think Josh would hold another Dogs of Doom concert?'

The girls stop rolling and giggling and sit up.

'He'd love to!' Luce gasps. 'I know he would. I'll ring him now.'

She reaches for her bag, but Sorrel puts her hand on

her arm. 'Luce don't, *please*.' She looks across at me. 'Look, it's not that I'm not grateful or anything, but I'm not really a deserving cause. The last concert was for people who are seriously ill. I'm not about to peg it. I just legged it 'cause I got in a strop, and I'm really sorry for getting stroppy, especially with you two.'

'But—' I start to protest, but Sorrel interrupts me by holding up her hands.

'No, honestly, I'd feel uncomfortable and, anyway, by the time Josh could organize the gig, Christmas will be over. If I'm going to go I need to book my ticket now, and I haven't the money. I should never have mentioned it.'

'There must be something we can do to get cash quickly,' I say. 'Something legal.'

'When I was little and wanted a pony I had a jumble sale to raise the money,' Lucy says. 'We had a trestle table at the end of the drive and I put all my dolls on it, do you remember?'

'I remember your mum buying everything on the table just to get you back inside,' I say. '*And* you never got the pony because The Neat Freak has a thing about pony poo. Even if we did set up a table in Mortimer Road I can't see us getting very much for some old jeans, broken-down shoes and odd earrings. I don't have anything valuable.'

Then I remember.

'I do! I've got the bling bag! Let's sell The Bag of Beauty! It must be worth hundreds. You can have the money for your ticket.'

'But you love that bag,' Sorrel says. 'You even went out with Pinhead for it.'

'This all started with that wretched bag,' I grumble. 'It's brought me nothing but grief the moment I got it. It was part of the bet, it lost me FB, it's too expensive to use, and I'm always worried I'm going to get mugged or smear it with a stray Snickers bar. Let's stick it on eBay and see what we get. I'd rather you had the money than it sat in my cupboard. We can call it Operation Chloé.'

'I really really appreciate it,' Sorrel says, her eyes looking softer for the first time since she came back. 'But by the time it's on eBay and you've got the money, it'll be too late to get a ticket.'

Damn! Why is it that every part of every plan I make has a flaw in it? It would have been so much easier if Sorrel had run away a few weeks ago and given me time to get my plan in place.

Lucy flicks open her phone.

'Luce, don't ring Josh, please,' Sorrel pleads.

'I'm not,' Luce says. 'If Mum bought all those things

years ago to help me out, maybe she can buy The Bag of Beauty off Electra now.'

As it turned out, Lucy's mum didn't want to buy The Bag of Beauty (too flashy!), but after lots of discussion and passing around of Lucy's phone to each of us, Bella's come up with a plan that I have to admit is even better than mine.

Bella will buy an economy return ticket to Barbados for Sorrel.

Sorrel has promised to come back after Christmas, live at home and start school on January 7th.

In the meantime, Bella will sell the bag on eBay and put the proceeds against the cost of the ticket. She's also going to auction some of her designer shoes and clothes, and stuff Luce and the boys have grown out of.

If all the money we raise doesn't cover the airfare, then Lucy, Sorrel and I have said that somehow we'll make up the difference, even if it means doing a paper round or washing cars, though clearly I hope it doesn't come to manual labour.

The only problem is that it's not only Yolanda and Desmond Callender who have to agree to the plan. Precious Oyedele, Sorrel's case worker has to too.

* * *

We had a quiet night with pizza and the telly on Monday. Sorrel didn't go to school on Tuesday either, but spent hours talking to social workers and other people with forms and clipboards and, according to Sorrel, serious faces.

On Tuesday evening, Mum cooked a roast beef dinner in honour of Sorrel's return, Phil dragged the Christmas tree in from the garden and put the lights on, after which me, Sorrel and Jack draped it with baubles and tinsel and things made out of cotton wool, glitter and egg cartons Jack and I have made over the years, and now, twinkling away in the corner, it looks very festive. The pile of cards that had been mounting on the dresser are now hung over pictures and wedged behind ornaments, and as I sit down to eat, I feel Christmas spirit has finally arrived at 14 Mortimer Road.

As has Sorrel's mum.

I can hear her bike being wheeled into the hall.

'We're down here,' Phil says, showing Yolanda into the kitchen. 'Would you like to join us?'

I see Yolanda wince at the lump of dead cow oozing blood on the table, and for a moment wonder if she's going to start a lecture on the virtues of veganism.

'Can I get you some vegetables, Yolanda?' Mum asks, getting up. 'Or a glass of wine?'

Yolanda shakes her head.

'I'm fine, thank you, Ellie. I just wanted to say, Sorrel, I've spoken to your father and he'd love to have you for Christmas, as long as you promise to come back home afterwards. No running into the sugar plantations or getting on a boat to St Lucia.'

'What about Mrs Oyedele?' Sorrel asks, wide-eyed. 'Will she agree to it?'

'It's all sorted,' Yolanda says. 'But just because we're letting you go, doesn't mean we won't miss you.'

Sorrel yelps with joy, jumps up and goes to hug Yolanda, who doesn't flinch, despite the fact she must be able to smell dead animal on Sorrel's breath.

'And I'll miss you too,' Sorrel smiles, which would be a lovely look if she hadn't got bits of bloody meat stuck between her teeth.

Yolanda suddenly looks distressed, and I don't think it's because of the sight of the meat. 'Can I just say . . .' She pauses, breathing heavily. 'Can I just say I'm humiliated not to have been able to help my daughter see her father sooner. So many children, so little money.' She gives an embarrassed laugh and buries her chin in the red scarf around her neck. 'Funny to think it's a bag that is making all this possible, after all I've said about leather.'

'Mum, it's OK.' Sorrel puts an arm around her mother.

'And just think, the animal that died is doing some good after all!'

I have to clench my bum really hard to stop myself giggling.

'Sorrel, we're going to look at how we can rearrange the house so you have your own space, maybe an old caravan on the drive,' Yolanda says. 'Longer term, Mrs Oyedele thinks we might be able to be rehoused somewhere a bit bigger.'

The neighbours are going to love that! I think to myself. First a funereal car and now some clapped-out caravan parked next to their flowerbeds.

'Thanks, Mum,' Sorrel says. 'A caravan would be fab.'

'Are you sure you won't stay?' Mum asks. 'You'd be very welcome.'

'You've all done quite enough.' Yolanda looks at me just as I'm stuffing an Aunt Bessie's yorkie into my mouth. 'Especially you, Electra, giving up something Sorrel tells me was dear to you. I've always thought you lovely but a bit shallow. You clearly have hidden depths.'

Chapter Twenty-one

It certainly is the season to be jolly!

Even though I'm peeling potatoes and am up to my elbows in cold dirty spud-skin water, and am slightly concerned that the mani I gave myself on Christmas Eve (a rather festive red with what was meant to be silver stars but turned out to be silver blobs) is going to flake off, I'm so happy I could burst. Actually, if I have any more to eat I *will* burst! We're not having Christmas lunch until four as Phil is working this morning, so after starting with bacon sarnies for breakfast, I've been grazing all day on chocolate and Pringles and shortbread biscuits, basically any carbs I can lay my mitts on.

This is going to be the best Christmas I can remember for years, I think to myself as I toss a pale-cream King Edward into a pan of cold water, grab another one and try to take the peel off in one long brown strand.

It's been nearly a year since Dad left home, a year on January 2nd to be precise, and I never thought we'd have Christmas as a family ever again. Even last Christmas *before* Dad left he wasn't here for the whole day. We thought the phone call he got halfway through lunch was because of some plumbing emergency, when really it was so he could sneak off and meet Candy. I should still be angry at the thought that he deceived us, but this year I'm not going to let *anything* get in the way of a fabulous day.

Sorrel emailed from an Internet café in Barbados to say she'd arrived, everything was fantastic and that she'd been stuffing herself with fried flying fish sandwiches which sound gross, but she said were really delish.

She stayed with us and went back to school for the last three days of term, and despite some heavyweight grilling from Claudia, Tam, Nat and Shenice, Sorrel never let on what had happened during her lost week. Like Lucy and her self-harm stuff, I expect we'll find out when she's ready to tell us. It was great to have her at home though, and we spent hours gossiping about normal things like hair and nails and telly and what I was going to do about FB.

Despite it not being environmentally friendly and still running on diesel, Yolanda fired up the Goth limo again on Saturday morning, and all the Callenders (except Jas), went with Sorrel to Gatwick airport. I went with Bella

261

Malone and Luce, and everyone stood in floods of tears as Sorrel walked through passport control with a smile so wide it could practically span the Atlantic. I've asked her to bring me back two shells from the beach so I can make them into earrings.

Josh invited Lucy to the sixth-form Christmas party, which was held at a hotel near the school on the last day of term, something that sent Claudia wild with jealousy as she couldn't get anyone to ask her, not even dodgy-eyed Naz. Luce is now in Ireland with the rellies for Christmas, missing Josh, who's probably missing his dad, but happy as they're texting each other like a squillion times a day. Before Luce left, they swapped leather bracelets so it's defo serious.

Jack and I spoke to Nana Pat and Uncle Richard in Edinburgh this morning and wished them Happy Christmas, and Nana Pat said Dad had pressies for both of us from both of them, which is mega-exciting.

Mum is happy because Grandma is here with Granddad, and Grandma seems to have recovered from her treatment for bowel cancer and they're both sitting on the sofa knocking back sherries.

We're not opening all the presents until everyone is here, but Jack and me opened one each first thing. Jack got an Arsenal kit bag and I got a bottle of Chloé perfume, which Mum said was to make up for me giving away the bag, but in fact is better than the bag as I don't have to worry about losing it or smearing it with chocolate, plus it smells lush.

I hear the low hum of Dad's van pulling up outside, just as I finish peeling the last spud.

'That's Dad!' I say as the doorbell rings and I dry my hands on a tea towel. 'I'll get it.'

I look at Grandma, whose face has assumed its Lemon Sucker look at the thought of seeing Dad again, and even though I'm not mega-religious, as I go to the hall I say a little prayer along the lines of: *Dear God, Please let no one get in a strop and ruin Christmas, and please let there be a pair of burgundy leather patent ankle boots under the tree.*

Despite what Yolanda said, I still have *very* shallow moments.

'Happy Christmas, Dad!' I yell, throwing open the front door.

'Happy Christmas, princess!' he says, hugging and kissing me.

I kiss him back, but am half eyeing the armful of presents, trying to see how many of them might be mine.

We go down to the kitchen where Jack hurls himself at Dad, and I check on the veggie count. I've done the spuds, the sprouts, the carrots and the parsnips. The frozen peas are in the freezer, the bread sauce is coming out of a packet, the stuffing's already up the turkey's bum, and the gravy is still in its carton. I've even found some carols on the radio. It's all mega-festive.

'You've done the presents already?' Dad sounds disappointed as he eyes crumpled wrapping paper on the floor.

'Just one each from Mum,' I say, nodding over my shoulder towards the Christmas tree, under which packages of every shape and size are piled. 'We're going to open the other stuff later, when Phil's back.'

'Season's greetings, William.' Dad smiles and nods at his ex-father-in-law and walks over to the sofa.

'Good to see you, Robert,' Granddad says, getting up and shaking Dad's hand so strongly their arms pump up and down. 'You're looking well.'

Grandma doesn't get up but glances over her shoulder.

'You're looking fat,' she says crisply, before taking another slug of sherry.

'Good to see you too, Dorothy,' Dad laughs. 'You haven't changed. But you're absolutely right. I'm going to start a fitness regime in the New Year. Next time you see me I'll have a six-pack!'

'A pack of six what?' Granddad asks looking confused, as Dad and I laugh.

Mum comes into the kitchen wearing her grey party frock and pearls.

'Hello, Rob. Happy Christmas.'

They don't shake hands or hug, just half smile and nod at each other. I can tell Mum's feeling a bit tense about all this, and for the first time I actually wish that I hadn't pushed her to allow Dad to come. She's looking a bit pale, a bit peaky, but then she has been slaving over a hot oven for the last few hours, wrestling with a monster turkey, and fretting over the cream not whipping for the trifle. She went for a lie-down earlier as she felt a bit dizzy when she opened the oven to baste the bird and hot air shot out.

'I've just been telling Robert, he's become rather chunky,' Grandma says. 'Speaking of which, so are you, Eleanor. That's why you'll be so tired. Carrying that extra weight around. Have you been eating all the Quality Street again?'

As she's had a go at both Mum and Dad, I wait for her to start on my muffin top, but luckily, although my grey jeans are low and my silver top a bit high, the gut overspill situation is camouflaged behind a pink flowery plastic apron.

Whilst I totter around in my spiky-heeled silver sandals, passing out (and eating) Twiglets and topping up the grandparentals' sherry glasses, Mum and Dad sit at the table, which I've set with crackers and a table decoration made out of Operation Holly Bush holly. It didn't have any berries so Jack made some out of modelling clay. Unfortunately, he'd run out of red, so he's made the berries pink, but it looks cheerful if not exactly Christmassy. And just for today, I've promised Mum that I won't kick The Little Runt under the table or strangle him with a piece of tinsel. I'll leave the physical violence until Boxing Day. It'll be something to look forward to in that awful post-Christmas slump.

No, I'm determined today is the day when the Brown household will declare a festive truce on each other. Peace and goodwill to all men, even ones that have been so unfaithful you've had to divorce them.

But now the big test is about to happen as I've heard the front door open and close. Any moment now, Phil will be downstairs in the kitchen with Dad. Will peace and goodwill extend to *all* men, even those who are sleeping with your ex-wife?

Phil bounds down the stairs, a broad smile across his stubbly chops.

'Bill! Dot! Great to see you! Happy Christmas!'

Instead of hand-shaking and lip-pursing, there's back-slapping from Granddad, and kisses from Grandma, and no doubt in my mind that Grandma and Granddad would rather Dad just crawled under the Christmas tree and stayed there amongst the fallen pine needles until the day's over.

'Happy Christmas, you two!' Phil beams at Jack and me.

We were still in bed when Phil left for an early shift so I haven't seen him. I don't want to upset Dad by showing Phil a public display of affection, so even though he comes over to hug me, I duck my head in a cupboard and pretend I've lost the gravy boat, hoping he won't realize we've never owned a gravy boat.

'Rob,' Phil says to Dad.

'Phil,' Dad says to Phil.

I come up from the cupboard now the introductions are over without fisticuffs.

'Respect for our sovereign please!' Grandma shouts from the sofa, and the room falls quiet except for the sound of the fan oven and the fridge, which has started to hum loudly over the voice of Queen Elizabeth II.

I lean against the sink and watch my family watch the telly.

Granddad and Grandma.

Mum and Dad.

Jack.

And then there's Phil, perched on the arm of the sofa next to Grandma and Granddad.

I like Phil, I really do. He's made Mum happy and he gets on well with Jack and me but, however hard I try, I just can't think of him as family. As long as it didn't upset Mum, if he walked out tomorrow I wouldn't miss him. I wouldn't wonder what he was up to or how he was getting on. I wouldn't make him a birthday card or visit him in hospital if he was ill. Phil will always be The Impostor to me. He'll never truly be a part of our family. He's just the man who happens to be going out with my mum.

It's hot in the kitchen and whilst everyone else is glued to the screen, I slip up the stairs, open the back door and, resting against the doorframe, look out into the garden.

It's starting to cloud over and it's bitterly cold.

I think of my friends having their own Christmases and wonder what Luce and Sorrel are doing right now. Thinking of Sorrel makes me wonder where Keesha is spending Christmas Day. I know that Sorrel said Keesha had no one who would miss her, but surely *someone* must wonder where she is, how she is, what she's getting up to? *I'm* wondering and I don't even know her.

'What you up to?'

It's Dad. I hadn't heard him come up the stairs behind me.

'Just thinking,' I say.

'Thinking what?' he asks, putting an arm loosely around my shoulders.

'Nothing much. You?'

Dad lets out a long, deep sigh. 'I'm thinking that it feels strange to be a guest in my own home,' he says, sighing again. 'I noticed some of those Christmas cards are still addressed to me and your mother.'

I have to try really hard to stop myself saying, *Well, whose fault is that?* But I'm *so* not going to spoil the day, so I just say, 'I don't think Mum told many people you and her split up. They probably just don't know.'

Dad's hold round my shoulders tightens slightly. 'We had some good Christmases, didn't we, when I was here?'

'We still can,' I say, trying to keep the atmosphere light as I can feel Dad sinking into a Christmas Day-and-alcohol-fuelled gloom.

'But now I'm a guest,' he says. 'I'm a guest and all because this time last year do you know what was in my pants?'

Oh. My. God. I *so* don't want to think of what might be in Dad's pants. I've seen him in his bright-red tiny Speedos so I've got a *very* good idea.

269

'My brains!' Dad says. 'My brains were where my boy parts are.'

Oh, this is just too much, having eaten a belly load of carbs and just before I tuck into Christmas dinner. No one should have to hear their middle-aged father say *boy parts* on Christmas Day.

Dad prattles on, getting it all off his man-boobs. 'My affair with Candy was pointless. I threw everything away for what turned out to be nothing.' He looks back at the house, light streaming from the windows as the National Anthem floats up from the kitchen. 'I'm so sorry, princess.'

I watch the clouds scud across the sky. It would be so easy to blame Dad for breaking up the family for the rest of my life, but I don't need to punish him any further. It seems to me that he's already punishing himself for what he's done and who he's lost.

'You'll find someone else, Dad,' I say. 'Someone who makes you happy. You won't be on your own for ever.'

'I didn't think you liked me having a girlfriend,' he replies. 'You hated Candy and Caroline.'

I put my arms around him, think *Gran's right, Dad is too fat*, and kiss him on the cheek. 'Maybe it'll be third time lucky on the girlfriend front.'

* * *

'That bird looks cooked to perfection, Eleanor,' Grandma bellows as Phil staggers to the table and puts down the turkey, golden brown and glistening.

'Smells gorgeous too!' Granddad says. He starts making smacking noises with his lips, which encourages The Little Runt to do the same.

'Shall I carve?' Dad asks.

He's wearing a gold paper crown because Jack couldn't wait to pull the crackers, so we're all in our hats except Grandma, who didn't want to wreck her hair.

'No, you're all right,' Phil replies, picking up a carving knife, and not exactly brandishing it in Dad's direction, but clearly sending out signals that as New Man about the house, *he's* the one in control of the kitchen utensils. 'I'll do it.'

With a flourish, Phil stabs a knife into the crispy skin of the bird's leg, and a jet of hot fat squirts up and hits him in the chest sending the table into fits of giggles.

I needn't have worried about everyone getting on. I doubt Mum and Dad will ever *really* be friends again, but it's clear they're trying to get along for Christmas Day. Even Grandma seems to have lost her lemon-sucker look when talking to Dad, but that might be because she's had lots of sherries and is starting to look a bit flushed and squiffy. And now he's sitting at the table, Dad's

271

melancholic mood seems to have lifted and he's helping Jack try to work out one of the plastic puzzles that came in a cracker.

As Phil puts the meat on plates, I hand around the bread sauce and dishes of veg, Mum hovers with the pan of gravy, sloshing it on plates and Jack begins to eat.

'Isn't there anything I can do?' Dad asks, putting down the puzzle and taking some stuffing, spooning it on to his plate. 'I feel I should be doing *something*.'

'You can pour some more wine,' Mum says. 'That would be a help. There's red on the side or some white in the fridge, both already open.'

'I want wine!' Jack shrieks with a mouthful of food, spitting some of it across the table.

Dad gets up and gets the wine, and offers it to Grandma and Granddad, both of whom nod enthusiastically at the chance of more alcohol, red for Granddad and whatever comes first for Grandma.

'Not for me, thanks,' Mum says, as Dad goes to pour her a glass of red.

'Do you drink white now?' Dad asks. 'You always preferred red.'

He tries to pour some white, but Mum puts her hand over the top of her glass.

'Nothing for me, Rob.'

'Go on, just a glass,' Dad presses. 'It's Christmas.'

'She said she doesn't want anything.' Phil's voice is so sharp, I look up from my veg-waitressing and notice he looks a bit annoyed. Maybe he's feeling the strain of having Dad at the table. It's probably just as well he's finished carving and put down the sharp instruments.

'I'll have some!' I say to Dad, sitting down and starting on my turkey and stuffing. After I got wrecked at my own party I've been totally off anything alcohol-related (liqueur chocolates don't count), but I fancy a bit of wine with Christmas dinner.

'I've never known you to refuse alcohol, Ellie,' Dad laughs, pouring me a thimbleful of white wine. 'Especially at Christmas. In fact, the only Christmas I remember you not drinking was the Christmas you were pregnant with Electra.'

I'm looking down at my plate, about to spear a sprout with my fork when suddenly the sprouts, the parsnips, the carrots and the spuds start spinning into the gravy. I try to focus on the turkey but it joins the vegetable vortex. Then the plate seems to spin away from me, down a long black tunnel. The only noise I can hear is the blood rushing in my head and my heart pumping. It's as if I've entered some weird third dimension or am about to die. Then the rushing and pumping noise in my head is shattered by a high-pitched, '*Are* you pregnant, Eleanor?'

It's Grandma.

'The tiredness, your bosoms getting bigger, being dizzy, not drinking?' Grandma ticks off the preggers signs, which now seem blindingly obvious. 'You're expecting, aren't you?'

There's no need for Mum to answer. When I finally look up, I see Phil holding hands with Mum across the end of the table. He's beaming, but Mum looks worried, tired and suddenly *very* pregnant.

'What's going on?' Jack asks. 'Why is no one eating?'

'Well, it was a surprise, but you're both going to have a new brother or sister,' Phil says. 'Next June.'

Jack shrugs and carries on cramming his gob with stuffing, gravy running down his chin. 'They'd better support Arsenal,' he says.

'We were going to tell you earlier, love,' Mum says to me. 'But there was all the trouble with the school, and then Sorrel going missing and we thought Christmas wasn't the right time . . .' Her voice trails off. She knows full well there would *never* be a right time to announce to the family that for the second time in her life, she's accidentally got pregnant.

'Well, I think this deserves a toast,' Granddad says, somewhat unconvincingly. 'To the new member of the family, and his or her parents!'

There's mutterings around me and I hear Dad say, 'To the new arrival!' his voice hoarse, his hand shaking so much there's practically a wine tsunami in his glass.

I'd have liked to knock back my tiny glass of wine, slammed it on the table and shouted, 'Fill her up!' the way they do in movies when they've had devastating news, but I can't move. My bones have turned to stone.

'Electra?' Grandma says after the clinking of glasses. 'Aren't you going to say anything?'

What's there to say?

What difference would saying *anything* make?

If I said I'm totally shocked at the idea and can't bear the thought of Mum having another baby it's hardly like she'll say, 'OK, we'll send it back,' will she?

It is as it is, whether I like it or not.

I push my plate away, get up from the table and walk towards the kitchen door.

'Electra!'

As I climb the stairs I feel a hand on my shoulder but I shrug it away, walk along the hall, open the front door and head out into the street.

Chapter Twenty-two

I just walk. Walk and walk and walk and walk.

I walk along the streets looking in windows, each one a tiny snapshot of Christmas Day. Some people are sitting around a table, others are slumped in front of a flickering TV, a few are washing up at the sink. There are Christmas trees twinkling in windows and plastic snowmen stuck to walls, and signs outside houses saying *Santa Stop Here!*

There are people out walking their dogs, kids on bikes, couples strolling hand in hand, groups of families blocking the pavement, ambling along, chatting away.

I just keep walking.

I walk past a row of shops, their shutters down, their insides in darkness.

The Chinese takeaway is brightly lit and open. For a moment, I stop walking and pause by the door, sniffing the smell of fried garlic. There's someone inside, sitting on one of the red plastic benches waiting for their meal, perhaps someone who doesn't celebrate Christmas or someone who didn't have anyone to celebrate Christmas with, or someone who'd rather have sweet and sour prawn balls than turkey with all the trimmings.

They glare at me staring at them so I keep walking. Walking and thinking.

Thinking about how I've just walked out on Christmas lunch, and about how cold I'm starting to feel and the fact that I'm stomping around the streets on my own, on Christmas Day, in ridiculously high heels and no socks, and that my mother is pregnant by her boyfriend and in six months' time my world is going to be turned upside down by the arrival of a screaming wrinkly rugrat.

At this last thought, I feel my chest tighten, my knees buckle and I start to gasp for breath.

Clearly, I'm about to die, in the street, on Christmas Day.

That would serve Mum and Phil right. They'd never be able to see another sprout without remembering what they did to me.

I grab the nearest lamp-post, slide down it and sit on the kerb, my feet in the gutter, crying, real double-snotter sobs, the sort where you have to take two gasps of breath instead of one and snot runs down your nose from *both* your nostrils. I know that I've double-snotted because when I put my head in my hands I can feel wet tears and snot-slime slide across my palms,

'No! Not there! Oh you daft animal! I'm so sorry. I think my dog might have cocked his leg against you.'

I look up, and towering over me under the street light is a man and his dog. Not just any man, but Duncan Burns walking Archie. The old pre-Mum-preggers me would have been horrified that Dunc The Hot Dad Hunk has caught me sitting in a gutter, leaning against a lamp-post in double-snot sobbing mode, possibly drenched in dog pee, but the new me is too upset to care.

'Electra? Is that you? Are you all right?'

'Oh, I'm fine, Mr Burns,' I say, wiping my face with one hand, no doubt smearing snot, as I try to feel round my sides and back for signs of warm liquid with the other. I feel damp all over so it's difficult to know whether I've been used as a dog toilet or not. 'Happy Christmas.'

'You don't look fine,' Hot Dad says. 'What are you up to?'

'Just out for a walk,' I say, trying to sound cheery. 'I'd better be going.'

From the way Archie's sniffing around me, I fear I might be in danger of being used as a pee-post again.

'Do you always walk about wearing a crown

and an apron?' Hot Dad asks.

I touch my thighs and feel PVC that I know is pink and flowery, and feel my head and realize I'm still wearing my cracker hat.

And then I start to sob double-snotter tears again.

'Electra, what's wrong?' Mr Burns is crouching at my feet and Archie's next to him, panting. I hope for Glam Doc's sake it's the dog that has the rank breath, not her husband.

I can hardly speak for sobbing and snotting and shivering, but eventually I manage to gasp, 'Mum's pregnant.'

I didn't want to go back to Compton Avenue with Dunc The Hunk, but when I refused to go back to Mortimer Road, he refused to leave me sitting in the gutter in a pinny and hat on Christmas Day. So the two of us walked along the darkening streets, him saying nothing, me just sobbing, and Archie stopping every so often to cock his leg against anything upright.

'We've got people here for Christmas,' Mr Burns says as we crunch up the gravel drive. 'My wife's family.'

'I don't want to see anybody,' I say. Now the sobbing has stopped I'm starting to think about smudged mascara, a snotty face and red eyes, not to mention the possible dog-pee problem. I've already taken the apron and the hat off, though that now exposes a naked and freezing muffin top. 'I'll just calm down and then go home.'

Hot Dad gets his key out, opens the front door and shows me into a side room just off the polished parquet-floored hall. 'I won't be a moment,' he says, and disappears.

This must be Dunc The Hunk's office.

The walls are lined with books and files, and there's a state-of-the-art laptop sitting on a sleek glass desk.

I go to sit on the brown leather chair at the desk but, remembering the possibility of dog pee, pull my butt back at the last minute.

I swivel round, trying to see my back and my bum.

I can't see, feel or smell anything but, short of actually taking my clothes off, I can't tell for sure. I *so* don't want Hot Dad to come back into his study to find me standing in my knickers sniffing my jeans.

To be safe I take the apron and put it between the chair and my bod, and sink into the soft padded leather.

What on earth has happened?

How come one minute I was sitting at our table, enjoying Christmas, my only stress being about the possibility of footwear under the Christmas tree, and the next, Hot Dad has hauled me out of the gutter and left me in his study looking like a tramp, not knowing what's going to happen and stressing over the possibility of dog pee on designer leather.

I look around to see if there's anything resembling a mirror, and am just about to look at myself in the silver laptop case when the door opens, FB comes in and closes the door quietly behind him.

For some reason the sight of him makes me start sobbing again.

He leans against the desk next to me. Although I'm having a good sob, I can't help but glance at his denim-clad thighs. Even through my tears, I can see they are good thighs, strong thighs. Must be all that cycling.

'I'm so sorry, Electra,' he says. 'Dad told me.'

I sniff and nod. 'I've just found out.'

'You must be gutted.'

'I am.' I try and assess the snot situation without actually sticking my fingers up my nose. I *think* it's drying up nicely, but does that mean my nostrils and face might start looking crusty?

'What are you going to do?' FB lightly touches my arm, and I feel a shiver go down my spine, although this is probably due to the fact that I've been stomping round the streets in December without a coat and am chilled to the bone, rather than FB's electric touch.

Before I can answer, FB says, 'Hang on.'

He starts to take his navy jumper off but as he does so, it gets caught up with the white T-shirt he's wearing underneath, exposing taut, toned and totally lush abs, proof if I ever needed it that FB is no longer a chromosomal catastrophe but someone with drop-dead gorgeous DNA.

'Put that on,' he says, handing me a mound of soft looped wool and pulling his T-shirt back down. 'You look freezing.'

I put FB's jumper on and feel instantly better, as if someone comforting has put their arms around me. It smells comforting too.

'Thanks,' I say, smiling.

'Do you know who the father is?' FB asks. He looks solemn but gorgeous. If I wasn't worried about snot-face and the circumstances were different, I'd pounce on him, or at the very least, throw myself on his thighs, which are next to me again.

'Phil,' I say, wondering whether it would be just as unacceptable for me to pounce on FB as it was for Jags to pounce on me and, if I did, whether FB would wipe his mouth in disgust the way I did with Jags.

'No wonder you're so upset.' FB shakes his head. 'That's

shocking. Even more shocking than Pinhead or Jags.'

'What have they got to do with it?'

'The father of your baby. I thought it might be Pinhead or Jags, but your mother's boyfriend . . .'

Oh. My. God.

FB has *totally* the wrong idea.

He thinks I'm sitting on a plastic apron sobbing in his dad's study, clutching a gold paper crown, my face covered in dried tears and snot because, 'YOU THINK *I'M* PREGGERS?'

'That's what Dad said.' FB sounds defensive and moves away from the desk. 'He said you said you were.'

'I SAID *MUM'S* PREGNANT!' I shriek. 'HOW COULD YOU THINK IT WAS ME?'

'Well, people are, and you've been out with Pinhead and Jags.' FB shoots back. 'You wouldn't be the first Year 10 girl to get pregnant.'

'This is *me* you're talking to!' I snap. '*Me*, who's never been out with anyone! *Me*, who got grabbed by a Spanish Sleaze Bag and groped by a dim-witted hoodie! How *dare* you think I'm up the duff?'

I get up to go and grab the apron. I don't know where I'm going, but I'm not staying here to be insulted. I can get that just about anywhere.

'You look amazing when you're angry,' FB says.

'Absolutely amazing.'

What is it about these lads? You spend months tempting them with the entire package: clothes, nails, glossy hair, dangly earrings, just the right amount of make-up and a list of witty and intelligent things to say, and then they fall for you when you're looking a complete minger and shooting your gob off.

'I look minging,' I say. 'A mega-minger.'

'No, you don't,' FB says. 'You look like a gorgeous Greek Goddess.'

And then he walks over to me, puts his arms around me and kisses me softly on the lips, just for a moment.

It's not a snog, more a snogette. There's no banging of noses or the sound of water going down a plughole. Unlike kissing Jags where I was just bored and thinking of Plunge It Plumbing Services, in my head fireworks *are* going off, not just sparklers and roman candles, but huge things that make massive bangs and send curtains of silver stars tumbling from the sky.

I'm so shocked I don't know what to say, so I say the first thing I can think of which is, 'I think I've got snot all over my face and smell of dog pee.'

'You've got a lovely face,' FB says, pushing my hair out of my eyes and kissing me on the forehead. 'And you smell lovely.'

I'd really like him to kiss me on the lips again, but forehead kissing will do, and the Chloé perfume must be masking any canine urine pong.

He lets go of me, sits on the desk chair and I wonder if I should go and sit on his knee but I'm worried that it'll look much too forward, and also I might have to put the apron on his knee first, which might ruin the moment. So now *I'm* the one perching my butt on the sleek glass desk, which spreads my thighs and makes them look almost as meaty as FB's, which is a bit tragic.

'So, if *you're* not pregnant, why are you so upset?' FB asks. 'I don't get it.'

'I told you, Mum is!'

'And that's upset you because?' FB cocks his head in a really cute way. I do hope he kisses me again. Perhaps he likes me with a snot-covered face, in which case I'd better start crying again soon.

'For a squillion reasons,' I explain. 'Because my life will be turned upside down. Because I'll have a new brother or sister and I don't like the one I've got. Because the house will smell of poo. Because I won't get any sleep. Because if I take the baby out people will think it's mine and I'll be a pram-face by proxy. Because—'

'And your mum?' FB cuts me off mid-moan. 'How does she feel about the baby?'

'Dunno. I just walked out,' I say sheepishly. 'I just got up from my turkey and scarpered.'

'You have to go home,' FB says. 'They'll be worried sick.'

I know they will but I can't go back, not just because of the baby but because, 'I'm too ashamed. I've ruined their Christmas Day. I can't face them.'

And then I get it. I understand why Keesha feels she can't go home because she's been away too long to come back. Either pride or stubbornness or just shame stops her from making that call or ringing the doorbell.

'If you don't go home, you'll ruin more than just their Christmas,' FB says gently. 'They'll think you've done a Sorrel.'

I nod. 'You're right,' I say to FB. 'I'm not happy about the rugrat but I do need to say sorry.'

'I'll walk you home,' he says. 'Just let me get my jacket and tell Mum and Dad.'

'I hope you told your parents it wasn't me that was pregnant,' I say as we walk back to Mortimer Road, hand-in-hand. 'They already think I'm a bad influence on you.'

It's dark and really cold, and there's frost glistening on the pavement and the car windscreens. I'm glad we're holding hands, not just because it feels lush, but also because it might stop me slipping on the ice in these tarts' trotters and breaking my neck.

'I'll put them straight when I'm back,' FB says, squeezing my hand. 'Don't you worry about *my* parents. You've got your own to worry about.'

We walk along the street, looking in windows, giggling at people snoozing on the sofa, wondering what percentage of Christmas presents will either never get used or be taken straight to the charity shop. This has been the best walk of my life, but now we've stopped a few doors along from my house, and as well as the imminent parental face-down, I'm starting to stress over how I'm going to take FB's jumper off without it looking as if I'm stripping or taking the top I'm wearing underneath with it. I've got Maddy's air bra on, and it's much too early in our relationship – if we have one – to start flashing lingerie at him, especially lingerie that is effective but a bit medical-looking.

'Keep it,' FB says as I grab the hem, saving my blushes. 'Think of it as a Christmas present from me.'

'Thanks,' I say, suddenly feeling incredibly shy and nervous in case FB kisses me again, even though I know I'll be devastated if he doesn't.

'We're driving to Northumberland tomorrow, to my uncle's, until just after New Year, but maybe . . .' FB sounds as nervous as I feel. 'Maybe . . .'

'Maybe when you get back?' I prompt.

'Yes, maybe when I get back we could see a film or go for a curry or something, or just walk the dog, if that's not too borid for you,' FB smiles.

'You're never going to let me forget that,' I laugh. 'Anything dog- or food-related would be great.'

'I could text you,' FB says. 'If you like.'

I do like, but neither of us have a pen or our mobys handy.

'Write your number on here!' FB says, going over to Dad's van, which is parked outside the house. 'Write it in the frost.'

'But it'll disappear!' I laugh, tracing the numbers into the white ice across the glass. 'I'll be lost in the frost!'

FB studies the passenger window. The numbers are already gradually fading, becoming wet and blurry.

'I'll remember it,' he says. 'Remember, I remember all sorts of stupid facts and figures.'

'So my moby number is stupid?' I tease, waving a frosty wet finger at him as he ducks and roars with laughter.

We both look at my house.

Light is streaming from the basement and the front room is lit, but the rest of the house is in darkness. However fun it's been here outside with FB, we both know I have to go inside and face the music, and that the sort of music I'm going to face isn't going to be a sparkly Christmas jingle.

'Happy Christmas, Electra,' FB says. 'Whatever happens, I'll always be there for you.'

And then he kisses me again, and this time, it's definitely *not* a snogette.

Chapter Twenty-three

I'd like to say that I was welcomed back into the household with open arms, tears and a promise of an increase in my allowance, but obviously storming out of Christmas dinner for a couple of hours doesn't have the same effect as going missing for a week and sleeping rough.

I was met by a furious Phil at the front door (having left my keys, I had to ring the bell), my plate of cold greasy Christmas dinner, a stony silence from Dad and a mound of wrapping paper as everyone had opened their presents without me. Jack didn't even seem to realize I'd gone missing and was playing with a toy shooting gallery, and Grandma and Granddad probably did realize but weren't worried, as they're asleep in front of the telly, mouths open, Grandma snoring.

'Where's Mum?' I say, wondering if it would be rude to open my presents straightaway, just to see if the ankle boots are there. If they are, I'm already planning on wearing them on my first date with FB.

'In her room,' Phil snaps, going to the fridge, offering Dad a beer and opening one himself. 'Trying to get some rest.'

'Mum?' I peer round her bedroom door.

She's lying on the bed, on her back, her eyes open, no light on, the curtains undrawn and just the street light outside illuminating the room. For one terrible moment, I think she might be dead, but on closer examination I can see her Mighty Mammaries rising and falling. The size of them coupled with gravity probably means that a lot of breast-flesh is actually under her armpits.

'Mum, I'm so sorry.'

I'm in the room now, hovering by her bed. It's not been made so she's lying on the crumpled white sheets like some giant grey whale beached amongst pillows and a fifteen-tog feather duvet.

She keeps staring at the ceiling. Perhaps the shock of my walking out has rendered her speechless.

'I didn't mean to storm out like that, I just did. I mean, I didn't think. Well, I did think, but about me, not about you. Sorry.'

Still nothing.

Perhaps she's had a stroke? Lucy's grandma had a stroke, and Luce said she dribbled a lot. I can't see any rivers of saliva running out of the side of Mum's mouth, but then the light isn't good.

'Mum?'

Finally she hauls herself up the bed, switches on her bedside light and sits propped up on pillows.

'I'm too tired to argue with you, Electra,' she says wearily, rubbing her eyes. 'I'm too tired of trying to keep everyone and everything together. I'm not sorry about the baby, but I am sorry it's made you so unhappy.'

She's not looking at me, just staring straight ahead, but unless she finds a closed wardrobe door fascinating, she's just staring into space.

'It was just a shock,' I say, perching on the end of the bed. 'I never thought of you and Phil having a baby. I never thought of Phil being in our family for ever.'

'It wasn't planned,' Mum says. 'Like you, this baby wasn't planned. I expect you think I've been a dimwit *again*.'

'A bit,' I say, half smiling. 'Just don't call the baby anything weird.'

Mum lets out a deep sigh. 'I'm not perfect, Electra. I get things wrong. What with the stress of Mum's cancer and the divorce and – well, things were all over the place and we got caught out.'

'Dad looked shocked, but Phil seems happy,' I say, remembering he was the only one round the table with a broad smile on his face.

'Phil's delighted,' Mum agrees. 'And Mum and Dad seemed to take it well. Jack's just concerned it's going to be a girl and not interested in football. Your dad, well . . .' She gives another big sigh and rubs her temples. 'It was a shock for him too.'

I stroke FB's jumper. I haven't taken it off. I *never* want to take it off, though that's going to be a problem for school and if we have a heat wave.

I think of FB and me, snogging in the cold outside Mum's window, and feel all funny.

'How do *you* feel?' I ask her.

'Tired. A bit sick in the morning. Dizzy when I look up too quickly.'

'About the baby I mean.'

Mum rolls her eyes and pulls a funny face. 'Same as I felt when I was eighteen and found out I was expecting you. Shocked. Scared. Panicky. Worried about telling the family.' She gives a little smile and then looks at me. '*And* excited.'

It hadn't occurred to me that Mum, in her thirties, might feel the same as she did at eighteen.

'How do *you* feel?' she asks. 'As if I didn't know.'

'Shocked. Scared and panicky as to what it means for me. Worried about being seen out with a pram.'

Mum gives me a quizzical look.

'They'll think it's mine,' I say. 'They'll think I'm a teen mum like Cassie Taylor.'

Mum laughs and I climb right on the bed and snuggle next to her. It's odd to think that actually there are three of us in the room, me, Mum and a sproglet.

'Will you have to leave college again? Do you think you and Phil will get married? Will he sell his house and move here or are we going to have to move? Is that why he's always working, for sprog money?' I'm bursting with questions.

'I don't have all the answers yet, love,' she says, patting my arm. 'Is this jumper new? Was it under the tree?'

'It's a sort of Christmas present,' I say. 'From FB. Frazer Burns? I went round there when I left here.'

'Is he your boyfriend?' Mum asks.

I shrug and the jumper brushes my neck sending shivers down my spine.

'I dunno. S'pose so. Maybe. Sort of.' I'm still not sure, though surely a snog and my phone number must mean *something*.

'I thought Frazer was the school geek. The computer nerd. The one you called a freak.'

'He was but now he's totally lush,' I say, shrugging again, just to feel my neck being brushed. 'He's gone from Freak Boy to Fit Boy.'

Mum and I both giggle.

'I thought it was that Spanish lad you fancied,' she says. 'I don't know. I can't keep up with your love life.'

'He turned out to be a sleaze bag,' I say. 'A greasy munchkin from Slough.' I snuggle closer to Mum. 'Nothing turns out like you think it will, does it?'

'Not everything,' Mum says, kissing my head. 'Sometimes things turn out better. By the way, Aunty Vicky called earlier to wish everyone Happy Christmas. I told her about the baby before Mum did. She was pretty shocked. Oh, and Maddy was gutted she didn't get to speak to you.'

I'm gutted that I missed Mads, but if I hadn't walked out I'd never have kissed FB.

'Can I ring her now?' I say, looking at Mum's bedside clock. Almost seven.

'They were driving out of the city to a friend's for lunch,' Mum says. 'Try her tomorrow.' She untangles her arms from me and starts to get off the bed. 'How about we go downstairs and I make some turkey sandwiches whilst you unwrap your presents?'

'*I'll* make the sarnies,' I say. 'Then unwrap the pressies.'

Chapter Twenty-four

To: Madaboutnewyork
From: SOnotagreekgirl1
Date: 25th December 21:53
Subject: Christmas Kisses

Hi Mads,

Happy Xmas! Très gutted that I missed u when u rang. Did anyone tell u why I'd gone AWOL? I'd stomped out because of the Phil et Mum sproglet news. Can't say I'm thrilled at what a rugrat will do (vom, cry, not sleep, sounds like me after my 14th birthday party!), BUT what I am mega-thrilled about is that after I stormed out I met FB's dad who was walking FB's dog, Archie, who peed against me. Anyway – I went back to FB's (his dad took me) and OMG! we had like a nanosnog in his dad's study, and then a proper mega fireworks and everything snog in the street (after we'd walked back holding mitts). Mads, he's defo a 5 on the Snogability Scale and a total Lush Lipper! When he's back from family duty after the hols we're going to go on a date. He's already texted me to remind me I've said yes to a proper date, not just a hanging-around-the-shops date. Tammy Two-Names will be green with jealousy as she was trying to get FB to ask her out (he said she was sooooo boring compared to moi). I can't wait to tell Sorrel and Luce (I wanted you to be the first to know). And as for Jags. Jags who?!!! Loser! Still you've got to kiss frogs before you get a prince! Enuf of me. What did u get? Where did you go? Any Xmas snogging? Spill! Spill!

Miss u loads!

Masses of Electraspecial love,

Electra xxxxxx

PS I got a fabby pair of burgundy patent ankle boots from Mum and Phil for Christmas. Lush!

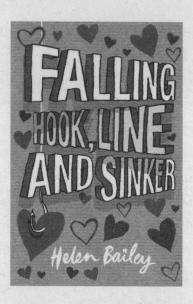

I am head over high heels in lurve!

I've fallen hook, line and sinker
for a testosterone-packed hunk.
He's cute, he's cool and he's been expelled
from school. He's also totally into me!

There's just one minor problemo: I already have
a boyfriend. I should do what's right
and walk away. But will I? As if!

I can be very shallow.

These are the frank and sometimes
seriously freaky rants of me,
Electra Brown. Welcome to my crazy world.